L. RIFKIN

THE NINE LIVES OF
Romeo Crumb

LIFE EIGHT

Illustrations by Kurt Hartman

Stratford Road
Press, Ltd.

Chapter One

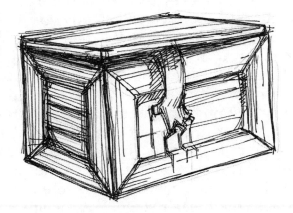

Darkness. As Grim awakened from his seventh death, he was surrounded by darkness. Nothing, not even his sharp, feline eyes could penetrate the thick black blanket of air. Alone and scared, he felt his way around the cold, wooden box surrounding his body. All he could hear was the ferocious beating of his heart as he waited, praying someone would come to his rescue. He knew all too well if he didn't escape soon, this box would surely become his coffin... again.

Grim's mind struggled to remember the events leading up to his seventh death. Despite his agonizing situation, he was able to recall several things. First, he remembered fighting his former friends, the Sticks, as well as his once again enemies, the Alleys, at the Hope Street

Chapter One

Theater. Next, he could remember Fidel's sudden escape and those haunting words he shouted at him, *I know who you really are!* He remembered the terror in Fluffy's eyes as, right before him, he plummeted off the theater balcony. On the flip side, he also remembered the feeling of pride in becoming a Troop member; the unexpected something to give him hope. Finally, he was able to recall his own brush with the supernatural as Ned the ghost pushed him to his deathly fall.

However the events unfolded, waking up in an empty wooden box was a horror he wouldn't have expected. Even worse still, he had no idea where he was. His last memory was falling onto the theater stage. Was he still there? Was he in the Fourth Corner? Were the Alleys involved? The Sticks? One thing was for sure, he wasn't alone. There were others around him. He could tell. However, there was one very different thing about them. They were dead.

The smell of a dead animal is very distinct. Over the years, Grim had learned this first hand, paw actually. From where he lay huddled, he could smell the decaying flesh of the unfortunate others. He imagined them trapped in the very same wooden boxes, crying out for help, clawing into the wood until their final breath. Grim had no idea how many of them there were. By the nasty smell, he sensed there were many. With his paws cupped tightly over his nose, one thought ran through his mind. *Will I be the next to rot?*

To Grim's great advantage, he was not at

Life Eight

the Fourth Corner with the Alleys, nor was he being held by the Sticks, who hated him as much as they would any Alley. He was, in fact, at the hoarder's house, more specifically, the backyard. Terrence and Miles, his trusted friends, had been standing guard outside the big, metal shed ever since Maxi, the human hoarder, viciously locked his box behind the large, heavy doors. Keeping with her hoarding tendencies, Grim had joined her growing collection of oddities in the makeshift tomb. Surrounded by piles of impromptu coffins, Grim took in a long, deep breath and waited for a miracle.

After what seemed like hours, Grim finally heard a banging sound coming from outside. He put his ear to the wood and listened.

"Grim? Grim, are you in there?" a voice called. The words were hard to understand, for the voice echoed and bounced off the shed's metal walls. He listened again. "Grim, are you alive?"

The voice belonged to Miles, his truest friend. Grim pressed his weakened paw to the scratchy wood and stared blankly at it, as if that would somehow help. "Yes, Miles, it's m..me," he mumbled. His voice trembled with fatigue. He could barely muster up the energy to continue. As always with each death, the body had a harder time returning to its former self. With a deep breath, Grim tried again. "Miles, it's G-g-grim!" His usual post-death stutter had also returned.

Grim waited with baited breath. After just a few tense moments, Miles spoke. "We're going to get you out of there! Just hang on, buddy!"

Grim crouched into the corner of the box. His body began to sweat, and his heart pounded harder. He had just shut his eyes when he suddenly heard a tremendous boom. The whole shed began to shake. His box nearly toppled on its side.

As the box rattled around, Grim pressed his two front paws against the opposite sides. He prepared himself for something big.

"One, two, three, go!" he heard next. A loud grinding noise followed, along with a cold rush of wind. The shed door was open. Terrence and Miles were coming in. Grim gasped for air. If they hadn't come, he would have surely suffocated.

Miles stood at the bottom of the large shed and peered up at all the boxes. They were arranged in remarkably neat piles, much neater than anything in Maxi's house. The smell of the dead animals quickly made its way over to Miles. It stung his nose like a wasp, shooting up his nostrils with a pain he had never imagined.

"Man, it stinks in there, don't it?" Terrence gawked as he crossed his arm over his nose. "That Maxi is sure twisted."

Terrence and Miles gave each other looks of concern. They knew that in all those smelly boxes were decayed, rotted corpses. Terrence felt a sharp pinch deep in his belly at the thought of some of his old friends, all of whom had gone missing at one time or another, all laying dead in that shed. He took in a deep breath of the heavy

 4

fumes and nearly barfed.

"So how are we gonna get him out of der?" Miles asked. "Those boxes look awful heavy."

"He must be the one at the top and in the front," Terrence deduced. "The last one she put in there."

Terrence was right. Grim's box was at the very top of four stacked piles. Being small cats, it was likely Terrence and Miles would have a difficult time getting him down. In fact, if they didn't succeed, they just may end up joining him in that shed. No doubt Maxi had plenty more boxes to spare.

Terrence paced back and forth in front of the open shed, which by some miracle he and Miles had managed to open with just enough force. Terrence chewed at the inside of his mouth as he concocted a plan "Let's just open the box from where it is," he said. "We'll never get that thing down. It'll crush us flat."

Miles peered up at the mountain of boxes. "But how we gonna open it? It must be nailed shut, don't you think?"

"We got the shed open, didn't we?" Terrence reminded. "We'll open the box, too. Just wait. You'll see!"

Terrence took another look around the yard searching for any sort of tool he could use to help pry off the lid. Being the hoarder that she was, Maxi had plenty of sharp, tool-like objects laying around for him to use. Any one of them would do the trick. "Let me just go up there and

5

check it out first," he said, staring up at the box.

"Just be careful," Miles said cautiously. "I don't wanna see any of those other boxes falling down. They could crack open and some yucky dead thing could pop out at us," he continued, feeling a chill creep up his backside.

Terrence put one paw to the cold metal shed. "Don't worry. I'm just going to check it out."

Miles watched nervously as Terrence cautiously climbed his way inside the shed and up the stack of boxes. Once at the top, he let his eyes wander around. The neatly piled coffins looked lonely and sad, reminding him of just what a somber place this was…a graveyard.

"Everything okay up there?" Miles asked. "Can you hear anything? Do you know which box is Grim's?"

"I don't know," Terrence said. "Let me check." He turned his head back and forth. "Grim, can you hear me?" he called. "I'm in the shed, Grim! Bang on your box so I know where you are!"

All of the sudden, a knocking came from one of the boxes. It was the top one he had suspected. "He's over here!" Terrence cried down to Miles. "I found him! I found him!"

"Good! Just get him out so we can close this thing again!" Miles looked up at the haunting sky. A wicked storm was suddenly brewing, and it was only a matter of time before it was ready to unleash.

Terrence stepped onto Grim's box as cold

air zipped through his fur like a fast moving train. The wind howled, and the sky seemed to groan. "Grim, I'm going to get you out!" he cried over the rush of the building storm. "Just hang on! It won't be long!"

"Do you need any tools?" Miles yelled. The wind was getting louder and louder, and he knew Terrence would have a hard time hearing him. "I said, do you need any tools?"

Terrence quickly studied the top of the box. "No, I think I can do it!" he called. "It doesn't look like it's nailed very tightly!"

"Hurry up, out there!" Grim cried from inside his box. He had heard Terrence and Miles this entire time and was growing increasingly anxious. "I can hardly breathe in here!"

Terrence reached his paws forward and dug his long claws under the box's lid. With all his might, he pulled upward, harder and harder, until the lid finally began to budge. "I think it's coming up!" he roared. With his nails dug into the underside, he pulled and pulled until BOOM! The lid shot off like a rocket. "I got it!"

"Awesome!" Miles cried, watching the thick board whip into the air and fall to the ground.

Terrence peered down into the box. As some specks of light finally reached inside, he began to see a sad little shape huddled in the corner. "Hey, you're not Grim," he snarled. "Who are you?"

Grim realized that Terrence didn't know

of his true identity, particularly his physical appearance. "Terrence, it is m..me, Grim," Grim whispered. "I'll explain later, now would you just help me out of here? My body aches s..something awful."

Terrence stared down at Miles with a look of confusion. Miles understood that look. "It's okay!" he called up to Terrence. "He is who he said he is!" Miles remembered seeing Grim awaken from his sixth death behind City Church. All healed, Grim was actually Romeo, a familiar Stick. After Romeo explained his situation to Miles, that he was not going back to the Sticks, that he had to remain with the Alleys as Grim, Miles agreed to help him 'look the part'. He knew that once Grim was out of that box, he'd once again be helping him, a task he was not looking forward to.

Outside, the wind picked up even more. The clouds were swirling darker. Surely it would pour. It was just a matter of time. Hesitantly, Terrence reached out his paw for Grim to take hold. As he did, a single drop of rain pelted down on the top of the shed. Terrence looked out and saw lightning flash across the sky with a loud zap! "Come on, this is it! Take my paw and let's go!"

Feeling a gush of relief, Grim lifted his head and stood up. He had been crouched in that small, wooden box for hours. His legs felt as if they would collapse beneath him.

Terrence waited anxiously as Grim took

his sweet time working out the kinks of his sore body. He arched his back to the sky and then brought it slowly back down again. Then he purred. Stretching felt good, but good or not, they needed to get out of there. If Maxi happened to come outside, she would surely slam them both in, dead or not. As much as she supposedly loved her pets, her diseased brain led her to strange and morbid behaviors.

"Grim, take my paw!" Terrence insisted. "I'll get you out. If Maxi finds us, there's no telling what she'll do!" Terrence reached his paw closer to Grim. A few more raindrops fell, making Terrence all the more nervous. The sky was teasing him mercilessly.

Grim poked his head out of the box. Until that very moment, he hadn't known he was in a shed at all. Cautiously, he crawled out of his prison. The rotten stench of the others became stronger. With a glance at Terrence, he hopped onto the box beside him and did a three-sixty. "They're all dead in there," he mumbled to himself.

"What was that?" Terrence asked, keeping a sharp eye on the dark rain clouds. "What did you say, Grim?"

"I said they're all dead in there, all of them." Grim seemed to stare off into space as his eyes filled with the morbid reality of the situation. "I wonder who they were," he whispered. "Maybe someone I knew. Maybe someone I fought."

Chapter One

From down below, Miles could sense the intensity Grim was feeling. If he didn't act soon, Grim would most likely slip into a deep depression. "Come on, Grim," Miles called up. "Let's get you down. You don't wanna stay in der. Besides, this wind is gonna knock me down! Now, grab Terrence's paw and come on out. You must be hungry, ain't ya?"

Grim stared blankly at Miles for what seemed like an eternity. Finally, something snapped. "Hungry, yes, I am hungry," he uttered. Looking over at Terrence he added, "Come on, I'm ready."

Terrence nodded, and together they climbed down the pile of boxes and out the shed. "That was easier than I thought," Miles sighed. "A cinch."

Grim gazed at them in a trance-like state. "She's a monster," he said. "A real live monster."

"Who's a monster, Grim?" Terrence asked. "Who?"

"Maxi, that's who!" Grim snapped. "What kind of a person keeps a bunch of dead animals in their backyard?"

"A monster, that's who," Miles added.

"You sure got that right, my friend," Terrence went on. "A monster is exactly what she is. Still, after watching her all this time I've come to understand that she really is a good person. She's just a little sick, that's all."

"A *little* sick? I'd say a lot." Grim stepped away and shook his head. "Weird, just weird,"

 10

he mumbled to himself.

Miles nodded in agreement then motioned to Terrence. "Hey, let's close that shed up again. We don't wants Maxi getting suspicious."

"Right," Terrence agreed.

Grim stretched his legs, bending them in every possible direction as he watched Terrence slowly close the shed. Just as it was nearly shut, they heard a garbled, muffled sound, almost like a voice.

"Hey fellas, did you hear that?" Grim asked, holding out his paw to stop Terrence from closing the door. "I think someone else is in there."

Miles squinted his eyes together. "What? You think someone's in der?" he cried. "Who?"

"I don't know," Grim went on. "I think I heard someone."

"Well, I didn't hear no one," Terrence said. "Let's close this thing up and be done with it."

Terrence pushed his body up to the shed door to shut it tight, when the slightest hint of a voice spilled from inside.

"Wait, I think I heard it that time!" Miles cried.

"Me too," Terrence agreed. "I think you're right! I think there is someone in there!"

Grim, Miles, and Terrence all huddled together in front of the open shed. They leaned their heads toward the stack of boxes and each cupped an ear in his paw. Sure enough, there was that sound again.

Chapter One

"What do we do now?" Terrence yelled over the increasingly loud winds. "How do we get him out?"

Grim looked up into the angry sky. He knew a big storm was only minutes away. "Come on," he ordered, "let's figure out which box it's coming from then go from there. Okay?"

"Got it," Miles agreed. They quickly scurried around, searching for whoever or whatever was in there. Grim's body had clicked back into action, and so he joined the other two on the search.

"Check every box!" Grim cried. "I know what it's like in there! We have to get them out, whoever they are!"

"You stay on the ground," Terrence insisted. "You've got to heal! Just keep watch for Maxi! Stay there!"

Reluctantly, Grim sat in the wet dirt and waited. As the others frantically pawed at all the wooden boxes, they shared the same troublesome thought, what if whoever was alive in there was somebody they wanted dead?

"I can't think of anyone else who's bit it lately," Terrence said, thinking of Maxi and her strange habit of keeping her dead pets. "You were the only one, Grim!"

"Whoever it is couldn't have been in there long," Grim concluded. "No one would survive more than a few days in those boxes. No one." He shuddered at the thought of being back in that box. Of all the horrible things he had been through, that box had been one of the worst.

As they clawed some more, a muffled noise got their attention again. "Help, I'm in here!" rang the voice. "Help me, please! I can't take much more of this!"

"My gosh, did you hear that?" Terrence shouted.

"Yes, clear as a bell!" Miles cried. "He's back der somewhere!" Miles rushed toward the rear of the shed, whipping his head back and forth. "Where is he? Which box?"

"This one! Please hurry!" the voice shouted once again.

"Over there!" Terrence yelled, pointing to the farthest box at the top of the heap. "I'm sure of it!"

Still weak and out of sorts, Grim watched from just outside, checking and rechecking for signs of Maxi. For now, all was clear.

Terrence leapt on top of the box he believed to be the one. "Yep, this is it!" he exclaimed. "I can feel him banging in there!"

Miles followed in a flash, while Grim watched anxiously from the ground. "How are you gonna get him out?" Grim shouted.

"The same way we got you out!" Terrence roared.

Just as he did before, Terrence and now Miles dug their claws under the heavy wooden lid. With all their strength, they pulled and tugged until the lid finally began to budge. They could feel it scrape beneath their blood-pulsing paws.

Chapter One

"Please hurry!" called the voice from inside. Already it was sounding weaker than it had just moments earlier. "Please…"

"Hurry, Miles! Hurry!" Terrence screeched.

"What's going on up there?" Grim hollered. "Did you find someone?"

"Just another few seconds…," Terrence roared, his voice muffled from the strenuous pull. "I think…yes, I've got it!"

Miles and Terrence flew backwards as the lid of the box flung off its base. Terrence landed flat on his bottom, while Miles did a mid-air flip and fell face first in the dirt. Grim rushed over to him.

"You okay?" Grim cried, checking Miles for the usual signs of injury or death. "That was quite a fall!"

Miles lifted his head just as the sky cracked open with rain. It was a cold rain, colder than most.

"Yeah, I'm okay," Miles mumbled. A bit wobbly, he got up on all fours and shook the dirt from his fur. Both he and Grim turned and looked up at Terrence as the rain quickly grew heavier.

"Well? Who's there?" Grim shouted over the whoosh and rumble of the wind.

From the top of the box mountain, Terrence hesitantly leaned over the opened casket. It was dark inside. Too dark to see just yet. Terrence's heart beat rapidly, and his breath was short. Anyone could be in that box. Anyone or anything.

As Terrence leaned in further, Miles and Grim stood nervously on the edge of their paws, little bits of icy rain pelting their heads. And then finally, after what seemed like an eternity, something moved.

A lone paw reached out and clung to the side. Its sharp claws dug into the wood like little knives. Grim jumped at the sight. Terrence leapt back. The paw slowly slithered in, leaving a pattern of scratches in the wood. A slight smear of blood remained.

Everyone was very silent, awaiting… something. Then, feeling brave, Terrence leaned forward again and stuck his head deeply into the box. "Are you all right in there?" he called. No one answered. "I said, are you all right?"

Miles slowly backed his way into the shadows. Grim stood tall in the rain, watching. Then, in a sudden move, the cat stood up. On it's hind legs, it grasped the edge of the box with his front paws. Terrence leapt back.

"Are you okay, fella?" Terrence asked. Miles moved closer, and Grim stretched as far as he could. The cat was dark, thin, and weathered. Its eyes were empty.

"I…I just…thank you," the cat whispered with every ounce of strength he had before collapsing back down.

Grim paused. "Is he dead?" he shouted to the others. He hated being on the ground, but his body just wasn't ready to make the climb back up into that shed.

Terrence sat up tall. "Not sure!" He put his head into the box once again. It seemed an eternity before he stood up and confirmed everyone's suspicions. "He's dead!"

"Who is he?" Miles asked, standing stiffly nearby. "Do you recognize him?"

"I'm not sure," Terrence called back. "He's far too sickly to tell."

"Do you think he was a niner?" Grim hollered. "Do you think he'll come back to life?"

Terrence rubbed his paw along the inside of the wooden box. Hundreds of deep grooves and scratches etched around the entire thing. Bravely he reached for one of the cat's paws. It dangled like a limp doll. He stared down and noticed how sharp and fine his claws were, a sure-fire sign he had already died and come back to life. "This cat died several times in this box," he concluded. "It's obvious he's dead for good."

From outside, Grim still stood in the pelting rain. Its intensity was increasing, and most surprising, it was starting to hail. "Fine! Just leave him and let's find some cover! There's ice falling from the sky, and there's only so much more I can take!"

Tossing the lifeless paw back into the box, Terrence motioned to Miles, and the two of them climbed their way out. Glancing back at the opened box, Miles began to push on the shed door. It must be closed or Maxi, the hoarder, will know they were there.

Terrence helped Miles. With a loud boom, the door was locked. All three cats felt a sudden pinch deep in their souls as the reality of what they had just seen hit them hard. Grim breathed in a sigh of relief knowing he had narrowly escaped being another victim of Maxi's death chamber.

"Come on, this hail could kill us all!" Terrence called. "Follow me to the house! Let's get inside!"

Grim and Miles exchanged glances of worry. As bad as the weather could get, going in that house was never, never an option they wanted. However, being that the hail was increasing both in size and intensity, they had no choice. They'd ride out the storm in the hoarder's house, then once again, resume life outside.

Terrence led them up the back porch stairs, all of which were seriously cracked or broken and covered in more trash than a dump. Miles walked in first. Terrence followed. As Grim stepped on the final step, he turned and gave one last glance over to the tomb that nearly ended it all for him. With a mournful sigh, he entered the house. As he did, a two sharp cat ears peaked its way over the shed. It was Roger, his eyes full of wonder.

Chapter Two

Fidel bound into his Fourth Corner cave just as the sudden hailstorm began. Rushing down the hallway to his own private room, he called for Bait, his ever faithful, although dim-witted right-hand male.

"Bait!" he cried like the ravenous beast he was. "Bait, get in here! Now!"

As always, Bait lurched forward at the sound of Fidel's intense voice. Missing his call would surely mean an afternoon of punishment. Being that he only had two precious lives left, Bait wasn't taking any chances.

"Yeah, Fidel! I'm coming!" Bait hollered as he scurried down the hall. "Be der in a flash!"

Bait burst into Fidel's room with a spark of adrenalin still in his eyes. Standing before him was Fidel, body clenched and sweaty, heavy breathing and raging eyes. "Where have you been? I've been calling you for five minutes!"

"Five minutes?" Bait cried. "But you only just..."

"Oh, never mind!" Fidel barked. He unclenched his fierce paws and sat on the dusty ground. "Tell me, what's going on out there?"

"Uh, out wheres?" Bait scratched his bumpy head with his paw and squinted his little, beady eyes tight.

"Out in the city, you fool!" Fidel growled. "What's happening on the streets? What's going on with the Sticks since we left the theater?"

Thinking fast, Bait struggled for an answer. Fact was, he knew no more than Fidel did. They had both run out of the theater so fast, there was no way of knowing the status of any of the Sticks at this point.

"I think they's angry at us...?" Bait finally said. "I mean, dey didn't want you to leave, right?"

Fidel huffed, and then proceeded to let out a long, slow hiss of disappointment. He folded his arms across his chest and glared at Bait with a look of pure disgust. "So genius, you think they're mad, is that it?" he finally asked.

"Uh, yeah, I guess."

"Brilliant, Bait," Fidel sneered. "Just brilliant." He walked in slow menacing circles around him as he had done so many times before. "Of course, they are mad! They are always mad! I want to know more! I want to know what they are going to do about it!"

Chapter Two

Once again, Bait squeezed his brain for an answer, preferably one that wouldn't ignite Fidel's anger any further. "See da thing is, I'm not really sure what they's gonna do now, cause I think that maybe if they do want, no, I mean, if they's gonna do anything, then…"

"Oh, shut up! You're babbling!" Fidel slithered to the rear of his room and sat with his back to Bait. "Get out of here, and don't come back until you have some answers, got it? I said, got it?"

"Yeah, sure boss," Bait muttered nervously. "Whatever you say. If it's answers you want, it's answers you'll get!"

"Fine, just get out! I don't want to see you! I don't want to see anyone!"

With his tail lodged tightly between his legs, Bait hurried out of the room. When Fidel says get out, you get out, no questions asked.

Eventually, Bait found Max, Reggie, and the other members of the Silent Five, including the newest members Cheeseburger and Raven. They were all standing in the dungeon, that is the empty dungeon. While everyone was fighting at the Hope Street Theater, Fluffy managed to free all the prisoners. Charged and ready, they had joined the fight with Fluffy until the Alleys had finally left. Now the broken chains and cut ropes lay on the dirty dungeon floor as bitter reminders of their failed plan.

"Hey, what's everybody doing?" Bait asked casually as he sauntered by. As shaky as he still was from his little meeting with Fidel, he needed to always look cool and collected in front of the others. He was, after all, to be in charge when Fidel wasn't around. "What are you guys up to?"

The gang glanced his way. It was obvious they were angry. Standing in that empty dungeon made them all feel like the ultimate losers.

"This is a disgrace, a disgrace," Reggie pouted. "Dose Sticks are gonna pay! Pay!"

"Boy, if I had a nickel for every time I heard dat one," Bait chuckled.

"So you tink this is funny, Bait? Is dat it?" Reggie snorted. "You tink this is some kinda joke?"

"No, no, you've got it all wrong," Bait said, nervously backing away. It was becoming increasingly difficult to keep his cool around Reggie. He had become very intimidating. "Just saying, dat's all."

Reggie glared at Bait with enough fire in his eyes to ignite a fear in Bait he wasn't expecting. Truth was, Reggie had nothing but repulsion for Bait. Knowing how clumsy and incompetent he was made him all the more enraged. Reggie had always imagined himself as Fidel's partner, not some half-wit who could barely tell his tail from his nose.

"So, anyways fellas," Bait said, purposely ignoring Reggie's probing stare, "what's are you doing? Really?"

"Just trying to figure out what to do next," Slim said softly.

"What do you mean *next*?" Bait asked,

clawing at a large hole in his tooth with his longest nail, a nasty habit he had just picked up.

Jackal turned his way. "The prisoners is all out. We let them escape! What kind of joint we running here? Don't dat bother you?" he asked.

"Of course, of course, it does," Bait agreed. "But thinks of it this way. Fidel was a prisoner, and now *he's* out, see?"

"True, true," Reggie said, cringing at the sight of Bait with his claw stuck half up his tooth. "Fidel has returned, but the question is...now what?"

"Yeah, now what?" Raven interjected. "What's Delly gonna do now? If he don't come up with some sort of a plan, I'll kill da guy! I mean it!" Raven wasn't fooling anyone. As much as she had complained over the years, she was eternally devoted to Fidel through and through.

"Look, dis is a good thing. We's the winners here," Bait went on. "Fidel's outta the theater. We know where da Sticks is hiding. So we lost a few prisoners, big deal. We can always get more. I thinks I'll even go find me some fresh meat tonight!" he beamed. "Now, who's with me?"

"Naw, I don't feel like doin' much," Jackal sneered. He turned away from the group and headed down the corridor.

"Yeah, not tonight, Bait," Cheeseburger added. "I feel a furball coming up, and I kinda wanna be alone when it does." With his paw to his throat, he dry heaved and walked away.

Bait watched as one by one, the others left

the dungeon. With their heads drooped low, they each sauntered out looking more defeated than victorious. *Awe, who needs 'em?* he thought to himself. *Dey wouldn't know a good thing if it jumped up and bit 'em.* He dug his claw deeper into his tooth until it began to hurt.

"And stop pickin' at your darn tooth!" Reggie shouted from the other room. "It's disgusting!"

"Awe, shut up, would ya?" Bait growled back, twisting his nail even harder.

Thinking fast, Bait headed back to Fidel's room. He knew Fidel would be calling him in for an update sooner or later, and as they say, there's no time like the present. After a few brief moments, he reached Fidel's stone doorway.

Bait pressed his ear to the door. He had learned the hard way not to enter uninvited. If he had been a little more careful over the years, he'd have at least three lives back for this alone.

"Uh, Fidel?" Bait finally called, confident it was safe to do so. "Fidel, can I come in?"

Bait waited at the doorway in silence until he finally heard Fidel's booming voice. "Fine, get in here!" Taking in a long, slow gulp, Bait shook the sweat from his brow and headed in.

Once inside the small but important room, Bait found Fidel. He was perched on his favorite pillow looking quite angry. Bait looked Fidel's body up and down, reminding himself of Fidel's powerful muscles and intense, almost beastlike form. Bait felt the familiar shiver of anticipation creep through his body. Even after all these years of working by Fidel's side, there was no end to his intimidation.

After a tense few moment, Fidel stared into Bait's beady eyes. "So? What have you come here for?" he bellowed. "You have some answers for me or what?"

Once again, Bait gulped hard, feeling it fall with a sharp ping deep in the pit of his belly. "Sure boss. I got some answers."

"Well? Spit it out, Bait! I haven't got all day, you know!"

"See, da thing is, I was just hangin' out with the guys," Bait began, already feeling his heart start to swell, "and dey are very ready for some action. Very ready to do action and start action..."

"What are you talking about?" Fidel snapped. "I swear, Bait, all you seem to do lately is babble!"

"No, no, boss," Bait stumbled. "See, da guys is real happy and all dat you's out of the theater. Real happy. But I was just thinkin', cause you know I like to do dat sometimes. I was just thinkin' dat we just do like...nothing."

"Nothing! Nothing! What do you mean we do nothing?"

"Well, you's out, and dem Sticks is the ones who should be scared, so why don't we just go back to like da old days and just scare dem from time to time? Prance around, dat sorta thing until something goes wrong," Bait said, with an almost innocent brilliance. After all, he was right. There

 24

really was no cause to start up at this point. But would Fidel buy it? "If we need to go in and fight, we will."

Fidel puffed up his chest with a deep breath of dusty air. He stepped off his pillow and sauntered over to Bait, never losing his gaze. Seeing Bait squirm in front of him fueled his needs all the more. "Do nothing! That is your plan! Wait for an attack! Wait for something to go wrong! Have you lost your mind?"

"No boss, I was just..."

"Have you forgotten those blasted Sticks had *me* imprisoned in that wretched stench of a place, wrapped in wires like an animal?"

"Well, technically speakin' boss, you are an animal and..."

"Have you forgotten about Miles and Grim?" Fidel roared, fire blazing in his eyes. "Have you forgotten how they turned their backs on us? Left everything we've been working on and joined the other side?"

"Actually, it was Grim who undid dose wires and let you go..."

"Shut up! Shut up, Bait!" Fidel exploded in a fit of anger, seething and writhing in his own jittery mess of bubbling fury. His body shook with rage, almost to the point of an all out seizure. "Listen, Bait!" he snarled. "I'm not going to sit here and wait for their next move! No way! I'll tell you what we *are* going to do! We are going to surround that stupid theater twenty-four seven! They won't get in! They won't get out! They'll

Chapter Two

all starve! No one gets in or out alive, do you understand?"

"Yeah, boss, whatever you say," Bait smirked with fake enthusiasm. "We'll starve 'em, dat's what will do. It'll be great, boss! Great! Let me go tell da guys, and we'll get started right away!"

Fidel exhaled it seemed for the first time in several minutes and simmered back into control. He strolled over to his fluffy pillow and sat down. Still with a gleam in his eye, he watched with clenched jaws as Bait left the room. This new plan of his would be his best yet. Heaven forbid he didn't have a plan. After all, the word *nothing* wasn't even part of his vocabulary. Not now. Not ever.

Chapter Three

A small crowd gathered around Fluffy as the life slowly crept back into him. First his paws started to twitch. Then his shoulders wiggled. Finally, he cracked open his eyes as his chest began to heave up and down.

Candle stood over him like any good nurse would. She had been awaiting this moment ever since he plummeted off the balcony. As she watched Fluffy blink his way back into consciousness, she breathed in a long sigh of relief.

"Fluffy, are…are you all right?" The sight of him took her breath away. Their relationship had spun in so many different directions, she didn't know what to think. Still, seeing him alive put all her anxieties to rest. As he sat up and stretched, she watched him intently.

Chapter Three

"Yes, yes, I'm all right," Fluffy finally whispered, a look of bewilderment hung on his face. "At least, I think I am."

Candle filled the space between them with a warm smile. She nodded for the others to leave, then reached out a paw for Fluffy to grab. "Here, hold on to me. I'll help you up." Seeing he was all right, the others left the stage allowing them to be alone.

"Thanks." Fluffy took Candle's paw, and just as she said, she helped him to his feet. He rose to meet her gaze when a sudden flash of memory zapped through him. He turned suddenly and peered up at the balcony. His eyes searched for Ned, the ghost of the jilted actor. "That was a long fall," he said as if to himself, rubbing the back of his head with his paw. A sadness came into his eyes.

"Yes, it was," Candle whispered behind him. "But it's over now. You're all better."

"Am I?" Fluffy asked, once again staring into Candle's eyes.

"Yes, you are. Who was that guy anyway? You know, the one who..."

"Who cares?" Fluffy grumbled. "He's an Alley. Get this, he tried to tell me he was Mr. Gamble's son. Is that messed up or what?"

"What?" Candle asked. "He said what?"

"Oh, nothing. It's nothing." Keeping quiet, Fluffy took a few small steps around the stage, seemingly deep in thought. Of course, he didn't believe Grim when he told him he was Gamble's son. The only son who that could possibly be was Romeo, and Fluffy knew better than to believe such a story. With that out of his mind, his head hung low as he asked, "Where's Sox? Shadow?" He glanced up at Candle. "Are they all right?"

"Yes, everyone made it out of the fight without much more than a scratch," Candle sighed. "Sox has been at his home all this time, but we expect him to make an appearance today. I know he'll have a lot to talk to us about."

"I'm sure he will," Fluffy moaned.

Candle's eyes wandered away. She was beginning to feel more and more uncomfortable. Fluffy too looked away in awkward silence. With neither sure if they were just friends, or more, or suddenly less, they each tolerated their own nervous tension for as long as they could.

"Well, I guess I'll head home for a bit," Fluffy groaned, breaking the uncomfortable stillness that filled the room like a thick stuffing. "Sounds like it's raining pretty hard out there. I wanna go before it gets worse."

"Yes, please be careful, and you should rest," Candle said, careful not to look Fluffy in the eye. "After all, you did just…die." As those words came from her mouth, she realized how insensitive they sounded. Fact was, death was fairly routine for these cats, and while lives came and went, death was never easy. "Sorry Fluffy, I mean, well…I think you should rest."

Fluffy nodded, for he knew she was right. Turning away from her, he headed to the rear of the theater and out the back door, the very door he had led her through on their date earlier that week. The delicious taste of that Croque Monsieur still lingered in his mind, as did the feel of Candle's gentle goodnight kiss.

Candle watched Fluffy's tail disappear out the theater door. Standing alone on the stage, she decided to catch up with the others. Surely they'd want to know how Fluffy was feeling, even after the relief of seeing him awake and breathing.

Just as she was about to step off the stage, she suddenly heard a rustling noise from above followed by a slight creak. Her eyes climbed up to the rafters and spotted one of the stage lights swinging back and forth. After a moment, it stopped. Shrugging it aside, she jumped off as she had originally intended and set out to find the others. As she slipped away, a small, dark shadow hung over the balcony, then flew away and disappeared.

"Candle, is he okay?" Twinkle Toes asked, seeing her enter the dilapidated lobby area. "Is Fluffy, like, all recovered?"

"Yes," she said warmly. "He's going to be just fine. He went home for a little rest, then I'm sure he'll be back to help us."

"Cool," Toes said with a sigh of relief. "That's all good. All good."

From behind Twinkle Toes, Candle could see some sort of activity going on in the coatroom. It was only hours earlier when their greatest nemesis of all time, Fidel, had been laying there captive. Wound up like the beast he was in rusted, sharp wires, he had professed to Candle his desire for her to be his treasured queen. Unable to stomach even the notion, Candle kept her cool and brushed him off, always maintaining her inner strength in even the toughest times of need.

As Candle approached the coatroom, she found Uncle Fred and Mr. Shadow assessing the situation.

"Hi, gentlemen," Candle began formally. "What's going on in here?"

"We're just deciding how to clean this place up," Shadow answered as he turned to face her. "Fidel was in here all those days, just laying in his own stench. I can still smell him. It's making me sick, to tell you the truth."

"Yeah, it's gross in here," Uncle Fred snarled with a scrunched face. "I think he peed."

"I think he pooped!" Shadow cried, seeing a disturbing something off in the corner.

Candle rolled her eyes. "Is there no end to Fidel? Such a monster." She glanced around the small coatroom as thoughts of his evilness filled her head. Remembering how Fidel confided in her about his own fears was daunting. Until this moment, as she stood in the remains of his captivity, it hadn't sunk in. They all had been running on an adrenalin rush since his arrival, and they hadn't had time to really process the gravity of the situation. Now that he was gone, escaped actually, she allowed herself a moment to reflect on the last few days. Feeling a heaviness

Chapter Three

fill her body, she fell to her knees and started to cry.

"Candle, Candle, are you all right?" asked Mr. Shadow, kneeling beside her. "Candle, what is it? Tell me! *Tell me!*"

Candle looked up into Shadow's concerned eyes. Between sobs, she breathed deeply and confessed, "It's everything! Everything!" She peered around the theater through her blurry tears and felt the weight of reality fall on her hard. "Fidel's out there...again. To tell you the truth, I'm relieved."

"Relived?" Uncle Fred questioned. "What do you mean, relieved?"

"I couldn't stand having him here!" Candle blared with an alarming depth to her emotion. "It was making me crazy! I'd rather have him out on the streets than here." Taking a moment to catch her breath, she inhaled deeply. She wiped her eyes with her paw, and then continued. "At least in here I can sometimes pretend that he's not around, you know, if things get really bad. But when he was here, I could never escape him! Never!"

"I know what you mean," Mr. Shadow agreed. "When we were at the Factory, I felt safe, even from Fidel. The theater can do that for us again...I hope. Having him here, even though he was all wrapped up, would never allow us to relax. Never."

"I just wish he was finally dead, forever!" Uncle Fred confessed. "I don't want him anywhere."

"Well son, we'd all like that," Shadow said

with a tug at what remained of his old yellow sweater. "Someday, Uncle Fred, someday."

A loud clap of thunder echoed through the theater throwing all the Sticks into a frenzy. One way or another, most of them had to get home. With a storm like this, their people would be worried. The Sticks were so grateful for what they provided, they never wanted their owners to worry.

The Sticks dropped what they were doing, and with their fastest feet, rushed off hoping to beat the worst of the storm. By now the hail was coming down hard, and many of them found themselves ducking for cover every few steps. Back in the theater, Candle stood in the empty lobby. She was all alone.

Chapter Four

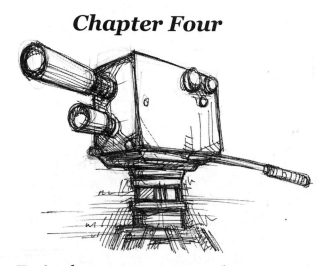

Early the next morning, the city streets were thick with a bumpy layer of ice. The storm had reached its peak late into the night, dumping massive chunks of hail in its wrath. It had been some time since the city had a storm as fierce or as relentless. Grim had never seen hail in any of his lifetimes. This had been a first.

Laying on a large pile of dirty laundry in the hoarder's house, Grim stretched his long paws over his head and yawned. He twisted his body back and forth, working out the kinks in his sore muscles. Nearby him were Terrence and Miles. They were still asleep.

As quietly as he could, Grim stood up on his four wobbly legs. His body was still tight from his last death as he had yet to walk the stiffness off. After another big stretch, he took

Life Eight

a step forward, careful of the piles of useless garbage that surrounded him.

Grim looked cautiously around the messy, cluttered room. His eyes scanned the vast wasteland of debris that lay like a roadmap to Maxi's diseased brain.

As much junk as there was, Grim was more set on spotting Roger, the hoarder's faithful hoarding cat. It didn't take long for Grim to remember what Roger had told him just before his recent death. *"I'm Fidel's son,"* he had said. *"If anyone's going to mess with my father and get away with it, it's going to be me."* Those words haunted Grim now as he peered around the room. What could that mean? Was Roger angry with his father? Did he know what a tyrant he was? Did he have any sort of relationship with him? Was he on his side? Those questions and more filled Grim's head in places where there was no room. So, with a pounding headache and the desperate need to get out of that house, he left.

Outside the sky had returned to its normal grayish hue. Dark clouds hung over the city, as they always did. A permanent threat. Grim shivered in the cold, chilly air. His fur blew in the icy breeze. The clumps of hail on the ground added to the sudden drop in temperature, giving the whole city something else to worry about.

Inhaling a deep breath of cold city air, Grim headed out for a walk. He walked alongside the house, landing himself in the front yard.

"Grim! Grim, where are you going?" he

suddenly heard. Turning around, he saw Miles standing behind him. "Where are you going?"

Grim didn't answer right away. He really didn't know where he was going. The thought hadn't crossed his mind. "I just needed to get out of there for a bit," he sighed. "I needed a walk."

"You're going like that?" Miles asked with a sharpness in his voice.

"Like what?"

"Well, like...Romeo," Miles said. "You still look like Romeo."

Grim glanced down at his body. Miles was right. He was Romeo again. To look like Grim he'd have to go through one heck of a makeover. As horrible as it was to have Miles literally beat him back into Grim, he did it once, he could do it again.

"Oh, what's the point?" Grim snarled. "Why can't I just go out like this? Who cares?"

"What's the point? What's the point?" Miles asked twice. "What's gotten into you? Are you forgettin' about Fidel? If he sees you, he'll know you're Romeo! You don't want dat, do you?"

Grim closed his eyes as he remembered Fidel's last words to him. *I know who you are. You haven't fooled me.* "Fidel already knows who I am. I'm sure of it," he sighed with a tightened jaw.

"What do you mean, he already knows?"

"When we were at the theater, he said, *I know who you are.* What else can he mean?" Grim turned and peered off into the murky clouds. "He obviously knows I'm Romeo, don't you think?"

Life Eight

"One thing I've learned over the years, is you never know when it comes to Fidel," Miles admitted. "He's a control freak, a mind control freak. He could say one thing and mean something completely different. He could just be messing with you. Why take the chance?"

"Oh, I don't know," Grim groaned. "I just don't even think I care. What's the difference?"

"I don't know how to answer dat, Grim," Miles said. "You know what's best...I guess."

"It's all so confusing." Grim sat on the cold ground. He stared at the icy road ahead of him. It almost looked pretty, glistening and sparkling as the sparse fragments of sun poked out between the clouds from time to time. The ice was so clear, it was almost blue. Grim knew all too well that by nightfall the ice would be brown and covered in oil heaved up from the deep belly of the city. Nothing pretty ever stood a chance.

"I'm just gonna go," Grim sighed, imagining how great it would be to have one sunny day. Just one sunny day. "It's early enough. I doubt anyone's out anyway."

"I'm not so sure I would go, but if you feel you're ready, by all means," Miles said with disapproval in his tone. "Maybe I should go with you," he suggested.

"Naw, I'll just go alone. I'll be fine, you'll see."

Miles shook his head. "I hope you're right, Grim," he moaned. "I hope you're right."

Chapter Four

Grim looked at Miles with dark but empty eyes. Miles knew it was wrong to let him just walk out into the city, but in some ways, it was just as wrong to hold him back. Miles nodded his way and watched as Grim walked down the street, quickly slipping out of sight. There was no telling when or if he'd come back.

Once on the streets, Grim was grateful for his claws. They dug into the ice with each step making it easier to get around on the slick sidewalks. Still, claws or no claws, the ice was clumpy and rough. It would be slow going.

The city was deserted. No one was out. Strange for a Tuesday morning, but after a hailstorm of that magnitude, businesses and schools had closed for the day.

The empty city put Grim at ease. He was, after all, Romeo, and more than anything, he didn't want any trouble. Despite his natural appearance, he couldn't bring himself to say, Romeo. Romeo, to him, was someone in his past, not someone he knew or related to.

Grim walked slowly down the unfamiliar sidewalks. This part of town was still new to him. He kept his head held low, knowing more than anyone of the potential dangers he could be in if discovered. He wasn't going to be stopped. His stride was arrogant and full of attitude.

About six blocks down, buildings and streets began to look familiar to him again. As Grim glanced around, he was reminded of both good times and bad. He walked past a storefront

 38

where he, Fluffy, and Queen Elizabeth spent one happy afternoon chasing mice. On the flip side, he saw a subway station and was immediately reminded of the tragedies and disappointments that followed the Vent City revolt. With a gnarling pinch deep in his belly, he continued on.

A little further down, Grim approached the familiar TV store that always had their televisions on in the window. This day was no exception.

As he stood on all fours, claws firmly planted in the ice in front of the large window, his eyes darted back and forth between the four televisions blazing behind the glass. Each one was tuned to a different channel, and on each one, news of the storm and its wicked aftermath played.

The farthest TV to Grim's left showed a man standing knee deep in ice, holding his news microphone and shivering. What one won't do to make a buck. The television beside it ran footage of a small car accident on a continual loop. The final two televisions seemed to be covering the same story although on different channels. It seemed interesting enough, so Grim took a step closer.

The noise from all four TV's made it difficult for Grim to hear what was being said, so he picked the one closest to him and focused hard.

"...The accident today involving a group of young boys is tragic," the newscaster said. "It reminds us all how fragile life is."

Intrigued, Grim stepped even closer. He squinted his eyes until he was able to read the small words at the bottom of the screen. *Four young boys*

Chapter Four

hit by hail as they step out of a movie theater. Only one fatality."

Fatality? Grim thought. *What does that mean?* Now really curious, he turned toward the other television covering the same story. He listened as the disturbing details unfolded.

"If you are just joining us, a group of four young boys out for a fun afternoon at the movies were surprised to find themselves in the middle of a hailstorm as they left City Cinemas. While most of the city's people jumped into cabs or down into the subway for safety, these four youngsters stayed outside."

Grim shook his head. *Idiots,* he said to himself.

"...The hail intensified, literally trapping the boys as they tried to find cover. But by then, it was too late. One young fellow was hit so hard in the head, he died on the scene. The other three are being treated at City Hospital for their injuries, some more serious than others. They have been identified as Homer Steinman, Baxter Jacklebaum, Dennis Crumb, and Malvie Fig..."

Grim's ears stood straight up. Dennis Crumb? Dennis Crumb? Could it be the same Dennis Crumb who raised him? His Dennis? *Two million people in this city. What are the odds?* Feeling his chest tighten, Grim listened on, holding his breath. *Please don't let Dennis be the dead one... Please don't let Dennis be the dead one...*

"Of course, as silly as it may seem, city officials are being blamed for this tragic accident as well as for the hailstorm itself, although they surprisingly have

 40

no evidence to support the accusations. Meanwhile, the bereaved family of young Baxter Jacklebaum are setting up a fund in honor of..."

It's not Dennis, Grim sighed. *At least it's not Dennis.* He suddenly had an idea. *City Hospital, the TV man said. That's where Dennis is! That's where I'm going!*

Grim stepped out into the street and looked the buildings up and down. True, he recognized where he was, but he was turned around just the same. *City Hospital...City Hospital...,* he thought over and over, trying desperately to remember where it was. Getting his head straight, he closed his eyes tightly and thought as hard as he could. Then, it came to him. *That way,* he remembered, turning himself north.

Grim tried racing up the street. After about two steps, he fell flat. "Hissss!" he cried, although there was no one around to hear. He tried repeatedly to get up, but he just kept slipping on that ice. Grasping it with his claws, he finally managed to stand up again, wobbling and shaking as he did. BAM! Slipped again. This comical scene went on for another ten minutes before he was finally on all fours and moving.

The hospital was a good five blocks away. At this rate, it would take all day. Determined as always, Grim would get to Dennis. He had to know if he was okay.

About an hour later, Grim had finally made it to the steps of City Hospital. His heart pounded from pure exhaustion. His fur was slick

Chapter Four

Life Eight

with sweat, and his body shivered from the icy temperature. Not a good combination.

Grim took a long, somber stare at the hospital. It was a tall old building. Its white bricks had seen better days. A few of the windows looked broken or cracked, but all in all, it wasn't the worst looking building in the city. Perhaps the mayor was doing something right for a change.

A stream of reporters, photographers, doctors, and nurses filed in and out of the hospital's two big front doors. TV crews had their trucks parked across the street. One crew was outside all set up and ready to film. Grim watched as the very reporter he saw on television grabbed his microphone and stepped in front of the camera and into a warm light being held above him. He stood on a towel to keep from slipping on the ice. Grim cautiously crept closer so he could hear the newscast. As always, he couldn't risk being seen. The last thing he needed would be getting thrown in City Pound. He wasn't wearing a collar, after all.

"Doctors tell me that all three boys will stay here in City Hospital," the reporter began with a wave towards the building, "for several days, possibly weeks. They wouldn't comment on the condition of the boys, other than to say they were serious. Some life threatening..."

Grim once again faced the hospital. He had to come up with a plan that would both give him the information he needed about Dennis

43

and keep him safe at the same time. Being a cat, he couldn't just walk into the hospital. Still, he had been in enough situations like this to be good at it. Perhaps even the best.

There was a small patch of dry pavement that seemed like a good place to stop. Quickly but carefully, Grim rushed over to it and sat down. Looking up at the big cement building, he searched for any possible clue to where Dennis's room could be. Unfortunately all the windows looked the same. Row after row of the same small, square windows. Depressing.

Grim stood up and was just about to check out the other side of the hospital when something bright caught his eyes. About halfway up the building were flashing lights. *That's strange,* he thought. The lights flashed on and off all in what seemed the same few rooms. *Cameras! Those are cameras!* It certainly made sense that Dennis and the others were being photographed in their beds. After all, Grim did see all those photographers enter the hospital. He watched for a moment as the lights popped on and off.

Searching for an entrance, Grim sat still and out of the way, keeping a low profile. He watched the people come and go, all the while half expecting to see Fidel or Bait or any one of his many enemies. Even seeing a Stick like Fluffy or Twinkle Toes could erupt into an all out fight. But with his eyes focused on that hospital, he was ready to risk all.

With his keen, warrior eyes, Grim spotted

his opening. Around the side of the building near the alleyway that lay beside it, one of the glass windows was missing. There was no doubt he could fit. The only question was when? Considering all the activity centered on the boys in the accident, Grim decided it would be best to wait until late in the night to make his move. So for now, he'd hunker down and watch for any sign of Dennis.

Perhaps just seeing the occasional news reports as they were being filmed outside would provide Grim with some sort of information. Even just a nibble. Feeling cold yet determined, he sat himself down out of the way of the crowds and waited.

About an hour later, just as Grim was ready to settle in for a quick catnap, he spotted a familiar face. Stepping out of a cab was none other than Mrs. Crumb. Grim's heart dropped. This was just the piece of the puzzle he had been dreading. The story on her face said it all. She looked grief stricken and pale. Her body was hunched over like someone who was weak and hungry. It was then he knew it had to be true. The Dennis he heard about on the news was the very Dennis he knew so very well.

Grim took in a long, deep breath and let it out with a sigh. He watched intently as Mrs. Crumb entered the hospital. She looked so sad. For the first time in a long while, a single tear ran down Grim's face. Soon both eyes teared up, and he began to cry.

Chapter Five

Candle wandered through the empty theater. She hated being alone, especially on such a night. The hailstorm lasted for hours. Her solitude seemed to intensify the sounds of the ice banging on the roof, making it all the more creepy and disturbing. There were also a lot of strange, unexplainable noises coming from up in the sound and lighting booth. Candle did her best to ignore them and focus on sleep.

The storm finally did end, and morning was in full swing. Surely some Sticks would be returning. As she eagerly anticipated their arrival, she let herself wander into the lobby. Staring at the coatroom, she was once again reminded of the devastating news of Fidel's return to society. She knew all too well it was only a matter of time before he attacked. After all, he had been

 46

humiliated and tortured right there before her eyes. She knew he wasn't going to just let that go. She knew he'd be back out there, maybe even looking for her.

Unbeknownst to Candle, Fidel's Silent Five were stalking the theater at that very moment. Their mission, find a way to secure the building allowing no Stick a way in or out. Fidel's plan to starve them, keeping them locked inside and away from their families and freedom, was all too enticing. His evil mind had no boundaries.

"Dis is too big," Jackal whispered outside the theater, peering up at the massive building. "Der's no way we's gonna be able to do this. No way."

"Yeah, there's a thousand windows and probably a million little doors and stuff," Cheeseburger added. "I say we just go back and tell him this ain't gonna work."

"Ain't gonna work? Ain't gonna work?" Reggie snarled. "Of course, this is gonna work. It has to!" With his eyes squinted down tight, he paced back and forth in front of the theater, stepping on chunks of ice with his meaty paws.

"Look, this is what we's gotta do! It's gonna be tough, but I certainly ain't goin' back to Fidel with that kinda news. He says that's the plan, so that's the plan. We'll figure it out, got it?" Reggie had a way sometimes of making the others feel like he was the one in charge. With Bait back at the cave, he wasn't going to miss this opportunity to boss everyone around.

"Dis ice is just ruining my red nails," Raven cried. Staring down at her chipped, red paint, she rolled her eyes in frustration. "I can't deal with dis. Tell Delly I gotta go take care of dis, 'kay?"

"Delly? Red nails?" Reggie snapped, storming over to her. "Is this some kinda joke?"

"What's da big deal?" Raven whined. "I just wanna..."

"This is your job now!" Reggie howled. "If you can't handle it, then maybe you and your nails should take a hike! There's plenty more where you came from!"

"Well, I never!" Raven scowled.

Reggie and Raven stood eye-to-eye, breathing fiercely against each other's hot, angry faces. With egos like theirs, neither one of them would be the first to back down.

"Come on guys!" Slim interrupted. "I think I sees some Sticks coming! We gotta get outta here, pronto!"

Sure enough, the morning crowd of Sticks was heading up the street. Walking carefully over the ice, using their claws to keep from falling, they made their way closer and closer to the theater.

"He's right!" Reggie cried, sudden panic in his voice. "Let's head back to da cave. Come on, follow me!"

Reggie, Slim, and Jackal, all veteran Silent Five members, maneuvered over the ice and headed back to the cave with a regal, stoic attitude and stature. It was not only in their job description to appear calm and mysterious at all times, it was who they were. Cheeseburger and Raven, on the other hand, shuffled along clumsily, slipping on the ice and embarrassing the others.

After what seemed like an endless walk, they finally made it back to the cave. Bait had been waiting for them. Cheeseburger wasted no time in telling Bait what he thought of this whole plan.

"Whadaya mean, dis ain't gonna work?" Bait cried as Cheeseburger told him the bad news. "Dis is da plan, see? It's gotta work! It's gotta!"

Reggie snarled at Cheeseburger. "Of course, dis is the plan," he growled, eyeballing Cheeseburger with a heavy dose of annoyance. "Of course, we'll do it. Don't listen to Cheeseburger. He is new, after all."

"I may be new here," Cheeseburger began feeling the effects of Reggie's insult swell through his body, "but I ain't new out there!" he cried, pointing in the general direction of the city. "Don't let dis body fool you. I've been around dis town plenty. I know what I'm doin'." He stared Reggie in the eye with a smug little smile, rubbing his doughy body and nodding his arrogant head.

"Oh, really?" Reggie cracked. He couldn't help but roll his eyes. "Like what?"

Chapter Five

"Well, where should I begin?" Cheeseburger said quickly, thinking hard for a good, juicy story. "Oh, der was the day when I...I..."

"Yeah, when you did what?" Reggie interrupted.

"I..uh..." Suddenly, Cheeseburger's body began to shake. He started to convulse. A weird almost prehistoric sound erupted out of him. He clenched his paws to his neck, and with one big heave, a massive furball spewed from his mouth. The others scattered immediately.

"Gross!" Raven scowled. "Dat was disgusting! You almost got dat on me!"

"Sorry, I just had a little something tickling my throat, I guess," Cheeseburger said shamefully.

"A *little* something?" Raven scolded. "That was like an entire rat comin' outta there!"

"All right, all right, will you two shut up already?" Bait cried. "Just go tell Fidel da plan is on. We'll get started like right away."

"Go right ahead, Bait," Reggie snapped. "You are Fidel's right hand man, aren't you? You go talk to Fidel. The rest of us will stay right here." He sat firmly down on the ground with a sneaky grin.

"Dat's right, Reg," Bait slurred. "You stays here. I'll go tell Fidel." Bait took in a deep breath and puffed up his measly chest. Truth be told, he was a little nervous meeting with Fidel. Even after all these years, Fidel never failed to

 50

intimidate him. Never. There were only so many beatings one could take and still stand comfortably in Fidel's presence.

After a short walk through the dark and musty cave, Bait reached Fidel's door. With his paws just inches away, he waited. He could hear strange noises coming from inside Fidel's royal chamber. Banging, clanging, huffing and puffing. Bait's heart pounded. He hoped against hope that Fidel was in a good mood, but in all his lives, he had yet to find him in a good mood.

Bait prepared himself once again and knocked on the door. The disturbing noises stopped. He heard pawsteps. The door creaked open.

"What do you want, Bait?" Fidel snapped with his deep, rugged voice. "Why are you bothering me?"

Bait paused a moment. His body wouldn't let him move. "I..I uh, just wanted to tell you dat the gang..."

"Spit it out already! I'm busy working out!"

"Working out?" Bait asked, suddenly gaining control of his voice and his body. "Why's you working out?"

"Why am I working out? Why am I working out?" Fidel howled, fire blazing deep within his beady eyes.

"Uh, yeah," Bait said, feeling uneasy all over again.

"Did you forget that I was tied up like a Christmas ham? Shackled and tortured! Treated like a beast!"

Chapter Five

"Shackled, really? Well, I just thought dat you was..."

"Oh, shut up! Get in here, now!" Fidel howled loud enough to shake the cobwebs from the rough cave walls. "I've got more work to do!"

Fidel threw the door wide open and marched back into his lair. Bait poked his head in. What he saw surprised him.

It seemed Fidel had moved his big mound of fluffy pillows to the side. In the center of the room was a large bag. Bait squinted, for the bag appeared to be moving. In fact, it was. Taking a quick step back, he suddenly noticed something odd about the walls. They were covered in blood, splattered blood. All over the floor, dead mice, some still whole, some not, lay in more blood. It was total carnage.

Bait took in a hearty gulp of fear and swallowed. "So, you redecorating or something?"

Fidel eyed him mischievously. He opened the bag by loosening a rope wrapped around its top. With his ratty paw, he pulled out a fresh mouse. As it dangled helplessly in his clutches, Fidel's breath grew heavier, and his eyes filled with fire. He started to swing the mouse over his head by its tail, keeping his intense gaze on Bait. With a loud whack, he thrust the poor, unlucky rodent against the wall. It slid down in its own blood and joined the other sad, little mice on the ground. This was a little too sick, even for Bait.

"Dis is how you workout?" Bait asked, feeling a lump well up deep in his belly. "How

 52

Life Eight

'bout I find you some nice weights, you know, to lift?"

Sweaty and hot, Fidel reached for another mouse, then another. He handed one to Bait and nodded for him to do the same. Nervous yet curious, Bait grabbed the mouse. He swung it around, as Fidel had done. The mouse cried and screamed, but it was no use. His time was up.

After a few more swings, Bait began to feel a certain sense of power come over him. "Hey, dis is kinda fun!" he cried. "I tink I like dis!" He kept swinging.

"Bait, just throw him down already! Throw the mouse!"

Bait was having so much fun swinging that mouse around, that he forgot what he was doing it for. Instead of whacking it against the wall, he sent it soaring into the air. He watched it fly up to the ceiling. Its little feet kicked as it flew higher and higher. Finally it reached the top, but instead of exploding in some dramatic scene of horror, it landed on a long pipe that was once part of an intricate water system. With its claws clenching firmly, the mouse tried hard to hold on. With every ounce of strength he had, the mouse pulled himself up and out of harm's way. Once secure, it scurried off and disappeared into the cave walls.

"Now look what you've done!" Fidel roared. "You let that one get away!"

"Sorry, boss, I was just doin' like you said!" Bait cried.

Life Eight

"Just get out of here!"

"But I..."

"I said get out before I get really mad!"

Bait left without having discussed the plan. He knew all too well what Fidel was capable of when he was *really mad*. He had enough bumpy reminders on his head to last the rest of his lifetimes.

About an hour later, Fidel emerged from his room. He was sweaty in a really gross, greasy way, and had little bits of mouse guts splattered on his fur. He was a sight indeed.

With his Silent Five standing before him, he firmly doled out his latest orders. "Males, tonight you will..."

"Excuse me, but der is a female in da room, honey," Raven brazenly interrupted.

Fidel glared at her menacingly. "As I was saying," he went on through his firmly clenched jaws, " tonight you will secure that theater. I want you to go find all the Alleys you can. That theater is too big for just a couple to handle."

Reggie smirked in Bait's direction. Bait pretended not to notice.

"I don't want any of you guarding the theater," Fidel insisted. "I need you guarding *me*! That's your job!"

"Of course, Fidel," Reggie nodded. "We'll follow you just like always. In the shadows."

"Stop kissing up," Bait whispered.

"Go to the Glitterbox, Smelly's, wherever you can find Alleys," Fidel ordered as he paced

Chapter Five

menacingly back and forth. "Tell them to go to
the theater and seal it off! No one goes in! No
one comes out!"

"What if dey don't wants to go?" Slim
asked. "The Alleys, I mean? What if dey don't
wanna do it?"

"Then they will be punished by me!
They'll spend their last days in my dungeon! I'll
let the rats feast on their flesh!" Fidel roared. His
blood boiled at the idea of anyone defying him.
"They don't get to choose not to go! The only
choice they've ever had was to stay among the
Alleys! They're mine forever!"

"Okay, boss," Slim agreed. "I'll let dem
know that."

Fidel rolled his eyes. He continued
slithering back and forth in front of them,
breathing heavily; deep in thought. Finally, once
his body began to simmer down, he released
them. "Go, go now!" he roared. "Get everyone
to that theater! Go!"

Like six perfect soldiers, Bait and the Silent
Five shuffled their way out of the cave. Mission:
find enough Alleys to surround the theater. It
wouldn't be easy; they knew that. Even Reggie,
who came off so confident, so arrogant, was even
starting to wonder. Was this job too big, even for
the Alleys? Full of doubt, they rushed out into
the city. First stop...Smelly's Bar.

Chapter Six

Grim woke up frozen solid. He had fallen asleep, and while he wasn't lying directly on the ice, the ground and the air were bitterly cold.

It was late morning, or early afternoon, he wasn't really quite sure. Either way, the sky was dark and cloudy. Looking down at his body as he stretched himself awake, he stared at his pretty fur. It had been a long time since he had seen his fur looking quite so nice. A good, long nap will do that.

Grim glanced over his shoulder. Sure enough, his signature diamond shape was etched into his fur. He knew if he planned on keeping up his 'Grim' persona, he was going to have to let Miles tear him apart. So for the meantime, while he was Romeo on the outside, at least for now, he still felt he was Grim on the inside.

Chapter Six

The hospital was all a buzz with people coming and going, just as before. The reporters were still camped out, waiting for any sort of juicy news on the condition of the boys caught in the ice storm. Grim watched them for a while as they sat by their trucks eating donuts and staring up at the hospital windows. Only friends or family were aloud to enter. To their great dismay, the reporters were forced to do all their work from outside the hospital. Over the years, the occasional reporter had managed to sneak in, disguised as a doctor or claiming to be a relative, but this story, being as high profile as it was, no reporter dared.

Before Grim would go exploring throughout the hospital, he simply had to get something to eat. He hadn't had a bite since before his last death, and if he didn't get something soon, he was sure to collapse from hunger.

Looking out into the street and down the still icy sidewalks, Grim went on the hunt. Unfortunately, he knew the juicy, little mice he so loved were likely hiding in the walls to keep warm. Sadly, that meant dining a la garbage can for Grim. Despite what most people might think, even cats don't like eating out of garbage cans.

Holding out for a good meal, Grim walked up the street looking for an open restaurant. Due to inclement weather, many were closed, but in a city like this one some businesses had to stay open. Because of poor politics, the city was in a perpetual economic slump, therefore, where businesses could open, they did. Every dollar counted.

 58

Life Eight

About a block down, Grim found a little café that was serving bagels, eggs, and other yummy breakfast foods. With his front paws stuck to the cold glass window, he watched with envy as the few patrons inside dined on delicious looking pastries and such. Being morning, there was a good chance it was too early to find anything good to eat out back, but there was always the chance. Making his way cautiously around the back, Grim found a row of garbage cans in the alleyway.

First order or business was to sniff out the alley for any unwelcomed visitors. Being behind a café, and a good one at that, it was likely that this alley was some cat's permanent home.

Not wanting to take any chances, Grim inched his way around, looking and listening for anyone or anything suspicious. Luckily, nothing stood out. When he was sure he was alone, he focused on the garbage cans.

The first in a row of three was the shortest. The shortest garbage can, for whatever reason, often had the best treats. With a big heave-ho, Grim leapt from the ground, bounding off his back legs with just enough of a bounce to take him to the top. Once clutched to the cold, metal rim of the can, he leaned over and peaked inside.

Scraps, he thought to himself. *Nothing but scraps.* Sometimes scraps were good, like a half eaten turkey and sausage sandwich. A rare find, but a good one at that. On the other hand, scraps often meant something so gross, even the most

59

starved and homeless stayed away. Once Grim found scraps of bacon fat and pork snout. At least that's what he thought it was. It looked and smelled so nasty, it really could've been anything.

Grim held his hopes high as he sifted through the meager leftovers. Finding a whole, unused pan of meatloaf or an entire salmon patty was always ideal, but it had been a very long time before he'd come across something as close to perfection as that. So far there was nothing remotely edible, unless you count some dried sour cream stuck to an old spoon.

Almost near the bottom of the can, Grim could feel his tummy growl deeper and deeper.

He peeked inside. *Nothing,* Grim said to himself. He hopped out, knocking the can over on its side making a loud crashing sound. None of the café employees apparently heard. No one came running.

To Grim's good fortune, there was an entire quarter of a chicken leg. With a huge, mighty grin, he snatched it in his claws and leapt back down to the ground. He brought the delicious find quickly to his awaiting mouth. Using his ripping teeth, he tore through the purple flesh, devouring the tasty meat. It went down a bit rough, maybe a little slimy too, but it was well worth the search.

Feeling full and satisfied, Grim slurped the last of the chicken juices from his paws. He rubbed his belly and smiled. As the much needed protein and calories started their path throughout his body, Grim turned to leave the alleyway.

Life Eight

Suddenly a noise caught his attention. He froze! Then he heard it again. Kind of like a clicking noise.

Grim carefully placed the bare chicken bone on the ground. This time he heard a rustling sound. He had been around long enough to know that someone or something was behind him. Nervous and scared, yet trying to be fierce and strong, he took in a long, slow breath and turned his head.

The alley was cold and creepy, as were most alleys. The usual odd shadows hovered around the old brick walls. A thick, black layer of dirty, rough ice covered much of the ground.

Grim squinted his eyes. He didn't see anyone yet, though he knew something was there. Tiptoeing toward the sounds, he pause as he suddenly heard, *click...click...*coming from behind one of the dumpsters. His heart stopped. He knew that if he was seen looking like the old Romeo, the Alleys would give him the beating of his life.

*Click...click...*it continued on and on. Grim contemplated bolting out of the alley, but his own curiosity wouldn't let him move. The question still remained, who was out there? Slowly and carefully, Grim inched closer and closer. The fur on his tail stood up on all ends. From his claws came sharp, pointy nails ready for action.

As he grew closer to the dumpster, the noise seemed to stop. Grim knew better than to walk away. He knew he had to deal with this head on.

Chapter Six

So, with another deep breath of cold, icy air he walked faster. "Who's there?" he cried, feeling his own sweat bubble beneath his fur. "I said, who's there?"

There was no answer. Grim stepped closer. Always on his toes, he gave a quick peek to his left, then his right, and then he glanced behind him as swiftly as he could. No one. Feeling his adrenalin starting to build, he called again, "This is your last chance! Tell me who you are, or I'm coming back there and I'll..."

"Wait!" a voice suddenly cried from the darkness. "Wait, Grim! It's me! It's me!"

Grim took a step back. He knew that voice. He knew who had been watching him. "Miles? Miles, is that you?"

Peeking from around the back of the dumpster was Miles's little face. "Yes, Grim," he said shyly like a child caught with his hand in the cookie jar. "It is me. Sorry if I scared you."

"Scared me?" Grim snapped. "You nearly gave me a heart attack!" Feeling his body calm, he was finally able to sit down and take in a real breath of air. "What are you doing back there? Why are you here?"

Nervously, Miles stepped out. As he did, his claws hit the ice making the very clicking noises that got him noticed in the first place. "I followed you," he finally admitted. "I just wanted to make sure you were okay."

"You followed me?" Grim cried. "Why did you think I needed following?"

Life Eight

"Well, you look normal, like Romeo again," Miles explained. "As good as that feels to you, it could mean trouble with da Alleys. If dey find out about you still being alive, they'll definitely kill you."

"I know, I know," Grim agreed. He dropped his head low and sat down. "I know you're right, but after being locked in that box, I just needed some time." He looked into Miles's big, brown eyes. "The thought of you, you know, helping me look like Grim was too hard to think about," he said sadly.

Miles put his paw on Grim's shoulder. "I wish there was another way," he said kindly. "But you got yourself into dis situation, and I think for your safety, you shouldn't be seen like dis."

"Oh, what's the difference anyway?" Grim grumbled. "The Alleys and the Sticks hate both Romeo and Grim. Who cares which one I am now?"

"I really think dat showing up as Romeo would be worse," Miles explained. "It would make Fidel feel like a fool. If he knew you had hidden your real identity all this time, living in da cave, being in da Silent Five, then, well, I don't even want to imagine what he'd do. What he's capable of doing."

"I know exactly what he's capable of doing," Grim said through clenched jaws as flashes of all the horror he'd endured over the years raced through his mind. "But I think Fidel knows who I am anyway. Remember what he said to me? *I*

know who you are. You're not fooling me."

Miles sat down. "Dat may be true, Grim, but then again, Fidel might be bluffing..."

Suddenly, a different voice shouted out, "It's not true!"

Grim and Miles quickly stood up on all fours planting their claws deeply in the ice, which was now turning to slush.

"I said, it's not true," the voice reiterated. Someone else had been out there watching them, but who?

"Who is that?" Grim called. "Tell us who you are!"

The dark shadow of a cat appeared from the farthest part of the alley. Together, Grim and Miles watched with bated breath. The feel of their sweat chilled them in the icy air. The shadowy figure crept up the alley wall, growing larger and larger until they finally knew who they were staring at.

"Roger? What are you doing here?" Grim cried. It was one thing to have his friend follow him, to keep a close eye on him, but Roger? What could he want?

"Stand back, Grim," Miles warned, shielding his friend with his arm outstretched. "Stay away from him. He's no good. I've always known it."

"Wait a minute, Miles," Grim began, keeping a steady gaze on Roger. "Let's see what this guy's up to." Gently pushing Miles's paw out of his way, Grim took a step closer. Roger met his probing stare with one to match, and the two sat eye to eye. "So, I'll ask you again, what are you doing here?"

Roger took in a deep breath and let it out slowly. He had been waiting for this moment all morning, and he wanted to make sure he said everything he had to say just right. "Like I said, Fidel don't know nothing about you. I told you before, he's my dear old dad, and if anyone's gonna get him, it's gonna be me."

"But what does that have to do with me?" asked Grim, his voice deep and serious. "What do you mean, he doesn't know who I am? How do you know?"

"Because I'm the one who led him off your scent," Roger admitted.

"Off his scent?" Miles cried. "What do you mean?"

Taking a dramatic step forward, Roger circled Grim as he cleared his throat. "You see, I figured out right away who you really were, Romeo."

"Shhh, keep your voice down," Grim snapped, turning his head quickly from left to right, searching for any more surprise visitors. "Someone could be here, you know?"

"Sorry, sorry," Roger said softly. "Anyways, it's like this. Fidel's my dad, right? Always has been. It's just my unlucky hand in life."

"So, you're not on his side?" Miles asked. Like Grim, he was confused as to where this conversation was headed. "You did say *unlucky* hand."

Chapter Six

"Yes, you've got it so far," Roger went on. "On his side? Never. Not since I was a very small kitten. Those were not happy times." He dropped his head and stared blankly at the ground.

"What was your childhood like?" Grim asked. He was suddenly quite interested in hearing about Roger's upbringing. Picturing Fidel as a father was beyond his scope of imagination. Incomprehensible.

"Yeah, do you's have any brothers or sisters?" Miles piped in, sharing Grim's sudden interest in the *fatherly* side of Fidel. "Who's your mother? As long as I've worked for Fidel, he never mentioned no kids."

Roger hopped onto an upside down garbage can. He took in a long, deep breath of icy cold air and let it out slowly. A foggy, little puff drifted from his lips as his eyes began to darken.

"When I was born," he began, "Fidel had just left Trolley Island. Have you ever heard of Trolley Island?"

Grim nodded. "I have. Mr. Sox told us Sticks all about the old days with Carnival, the original bad guy. He told us about how Fidel was Carnival's grandson; how he was born evil. Trolley Island was where it all happened."

"Yes, where it all happened for him," Roger went on. "For me, it all began right here in the city. At Stockwells to be exact."

"Wait a minute, Stockwells? I know that place," Grim said. "Isn't that where the..."

"Yes, the Factory. It was Stockwell's

 66

Umbrella Factory, your same Factory," Roger explained. "We all lived there. My entire family."

"So you lived at da Factory?" Miles asked, staring up wide-eyed at Roger perched on that garbage can. "Was there Sticks in it yet?"

"No Sticks. This was before the great fire," Roger explained. "The Factory was beautiful," he went on as a sudden twinkle sparkled in his eye. "It was a magnificent building. Gold elevators. Floors so shiny you could see your own face in them. Sure, it was old, but it was clean, like a brand new collar. The people who worked there would come and go during the day, making the umbrellas. At night when they all went home, us kittens would run up and down the halls, pretending that we worked there. I even made an umbrella once. It was a darn good one, too."

"So wait, I'm confused," Grim said. "It sounds like you had a good childhood. Sounds like you had a lot of fun. Why did you say there were no happy times? What's the real story, Roger?" Suspicious of everyone, Grim glared at Roger searching for some sort of clue in his eyes.

"Being Fidel's son, you have to make your own good times," Roger said solemnly. His tone had suddenly taken a turn for the worse. "He started the original Factory fire, you know?"

"What? Fidel started the fire?" gawked Grim. "Are you serious? Why would he do that?"

"He was crazy, that's why," Roger admitted. "I lost my whole family in that fire," he went on sadly. "It's amazing I got out alive."

Chapter Six

"They all died? All their lives in dat one fire?" Miles asked.

"Yes, all of them." Roger turned his head away. He didn't want the others to see him cry. In that moment, Grim realized how much he had in common with Roger. He too had lost most of his family to Fidel in one way or another. Perhaps he had Roger all wrong. Maybe he wasn't someone to fear. Maybe he was on his side.

"Fidel didn't want us kids," Roger said as he composed himself enough to continue. "I think that had something to do with the whole fire. He just wanted a quick way to get rid of us. Nice, huh?"

"What do you mean?" Miles piped in. "How could he not have wanted his kids?"

Roger stared up into the cloudy sky. After a moment, he shut his eyes. His face flinched as painful memories flickered like old photos in his mind. "The way he treated us," he began, "no one should be treated like that. No one." Roger gazed into the sky again with a strange look in his eye. "Me and the others, we all stuck together. My three brothers and three sisters. We had to. We needed to be there for each other, for the times when things got…tough."

Roger leapt down from the garbage can and sat between both Grim and Miles. For the first time, Grim wasn't nervous around him. There was something about his story that fascinated him. The thought of Fidel being someone's father was almost too much for him to take.

"Let me take a step back," Roger went on, sucking in a deep breath. "The seven of us, we were born in the coldest part of winter. I know that because my mother told us just before she... well, she told us that." Roger shut his eyes again. "So anyway, it was very cold when we were born. I guess we had just moved to the city. Fidel and my mother had recently left Trolley Island and all that it was behind."

"Yes, I've heard all about Trolley Island," Grim said again. "Carnival, too." Suddenly a light bulb went on. "If Fidel's your father, then Carnival is your..."

"Yes, he was my great-grandfather," Roger admitted. "I never met him though, but believe me, I've heard all the rumors."

"I bet," Miles sneered.

"Anyway, my mother was a good cat. She cared about others. She trusted others, maybe a little too much. It always got her into trouble."

"When did she meet your dad?" Grim asked. He leaned in closer. This story was going to be a good one. He could feel it.

"According to what she told me, mom met Fidel one day when she was just hanging around with her friends. They had finally convinced her to get out and have some fun. She had been in such a depression over her old boyfriend, Jimmy, they'd hardly seen her."

"Who's Jimmy?" Grim asked.

"Like I said, an old flame," Roger went on. "Anyway, they were catching mice or bugs, that

Chapter Six

sort of thing, when this group of males rushed up to them. She said they acted pretty tough, but were harmless enough. One of the younger ones caught her eye. That was Fidel."

"I can't imagine Fidel catching anyone's eye," Grim scoffed. "He's so ugly and, well, ugly."

"Maybe it's possible that back then before all those scars and things, he wasn't as revolting," Roger surmised. "But you know, even when he's lost lives, he still comes back looking just the same, like he had just been in a fight."

"It's weird," Miles said.

"Yes, it is," Roger agreed. "Anyway, mom had been real sad. You see Jimmy had just been killed."

"Killed? By who?" Grim asked.

"Who do you think?" Roger asked snidely. "It was Fidel in an unrelated event. Anyway, after Jimmy was killed, mom was real sad. I guess she kind of withdrew. She didn't go out with her friends anymore. She just didn't want to do anything. On this day, she had finally decided to join her friends."

"Were they Alleys? Sticks?" Miles asked.

"From what I remember of the story," Roger continued, "there were no Sticks or Alleys. In fact, I think that's why Fidel moved to the city in the first place, to start the Alleys. They couldn't all survive as one at Trolley Island, and so they began to divide. Something like that."

"Yeah, Mr. Sox told us that story," Grim said.

"Sox. Sox, I've heard of him," Roger added.

Life Eight

"He was friends with Fidel. They used to hang out."

"Yeah, I guess, but I don't think they were too close," Grim added. "I don't think Sox ever really liked him. He was, after all, much older than Fidel."

Roger squinted his eyes tight. "I just remember Ma mentioning his name. That's about it."

"Anyway, how'd she meet Fidel? Did she know he killed Jimmy?" Grim asked. Roger's slow story telling was getting him impatient. He wanted to get to the good stuff, not rehash all the old history that he already knew.

"Okay, so mom was out with friends in the city when this group of males comes walking up," Roger said again. "For whatever reason, probably out of pure vulnerability, she caught Fidel's eye. I guess he can be charming, as revolting as it seems."

"Hard to believe," Grim slurred.

"Yes, I know." Roger paused, a little too dramatically, and then continued. "Mom said that he was not a nice guy, right from the beginning. She said he was often violent, and he yelled at her a lot."

"That doesn't surprise me, but why did she stay with him?" Grim asked, anxious to hear more.

"I guess Fidel had mom convinced that she needed to be around him in some sick way," Roger said. "He had some sort of power over her. It was weird."

"So tell us where you come in," Miles piped up. "I wanna hear about your days as a kitten with Fidel."

"I don't remember much," Roger said. "Fidel was mean, very mean. He used to hit us kittens over anything."

"That sounds awful," Grim said, thinking to himself how lucky he was to have had his time with Dennis. "Oh my, Dennis! I completely forgot about Dennis!"

"What?" Miles cried. "What are you talking about?"

"I'm going to stake out the hospital," Grim continued. "He's there, and I'm breaking in tonight!"

"Why is he in the hospital?" Miles asked.

"He was in a hail accident," Grim said sadly.

"Who's Dennis?" Roger asked. "He some sorta cat?"

"No, he's my boy, my human boy," Grim explained. "I don't live with him anymore, but I always keep an eye on him. Like I said, he's my boy."

"Why don't you live with him?" Roger inquired.

"Because he put me to sleep, you know, the Sleepy Potion." Grim closed his eyes at the memory of that haunting day.

"Why would he do that?" Roger asked.

"It's a long story," Grim said quickly. "Look, I'm gonna go now. I might actually stand a chance of getting into that hospital. It's always easier to move around people when it's raining. They don't seem to pay much attention to us cats."

"Hey, wait a minute," Miles piped in. "What about Roger's story? I wanna hear more about Papa Fidel!"

"Another time," Grim added. "Look, I'll meet you fellas back at Maxi's place." Time was of the essence, and he didn't want to miss his chance to see Dennis. "We'll hear the rest later."

"Ok, ok," Miles agreed. "You better be back in two hours." He glared sternly at Grim.

Grim stared back at him with just as serious a face. "I'll try, Miles," he said, "but I'm not making any promises."

With a final nod, Grim walked away. Before he knew it, he was once again standing on the hospital grounds.

Chapter Seven

It was late morning. The hospital was still a flutter with activity. The story of the boys struck by falling ice had intrigued a city already plagued by drama. By now the press had multiplied, waiting for that crucial bite that could send them into super stardom. It was pathetic. Grim sat back and watched from a safe distance away.

After about an hour, Grim was nearly frozen solid. It was far too cold to be sitting outside. Besides, without a collar, he was a sitting duck, putting himself in danger of being taken to the Pound. He knew he had to leave the scene. Knowing he would be making his big move inside later that night, Grim decided it would be best to head back to Maxi's. It was almost time to meet Miles.

Grim turned away from the hospital

feeling as empty as ever. Dennis was all he could think about. He wanted to be with him, by his side. It killed him to be out of his life. After all this time, it hadn't gotten any easier. With his head hung low, he stepped onto the sidewalk and began to walk away.

Barely a moment had passed. Grim glanced up as he walked and soon spotted a group of Alleys far up the street. They were coming his way. Feeling the familiar pangs of panic, he searched for an escape. Dashing behind a large garbage can, he held his breath and waited.

With his claws dug between the metal diamond shapes of the can, Grim squinted his eyes as tightly as he could. *It's them!* he thought. *The Silent Five! Are they looking for me? Did they see me?*

Grim hid himself as much as he could behind a big stack of papers in the garbage. With his chest heaving up and down, he waited nervously for the gang to pass. Though he felt there was a good chance they didn't see him, the question still remained, what were they doing there? With his heart continuing to pound at lightning speed, he waited some more, not moving a single muscle.

Through metal slits, Grim could see the cats as they advanced toward him. Their serious and somewhat angry faces alarmed him. Even more intimidating, they walked together as one solid wall, trying hard to maintain their cool despite the difficulty of the slippery ice.

Chapter Seven

After a tense few moments, the Alleys passed him by. *That was close,* Grim thought. *They didn't see me.* He let out a tremendous sigh of relief as the Silent Five turned a corner and disappeared from sight. Seeing Reggie, Slim and the others brought out a whole new wave of emotion he hadn't been expecting. Being Grim and joining the Alleys had gotten him into quite a mess, and just the thought of what would happen next nearly made him sick. Taking in a long, deep breath of chilly air, Grim got himself together. When he felt certain it was safe to do so, he leapt back onto the icy streets and headed toward Maxi's.

Around the corner the Silent Five had continued on. Slipping and sliding over the ice they went, never seeming to be bothered by anyone or anything. That was the way of the Silent Five. To Grim's great relief, they hadn't been searching for him. They, in fact, were heading toward Smelly's Bar. It was part of the building next to City Hospital. They were on a mission to gather a team of Alleys to secure the theater.

"Where did you say dis joint was?" Jackal asked. "Ain't it supposed to be around here somewhere?"

"What are you talking about, Jackal?" Reggie sneered. "You've been there a thousand times. You know where it is. What's wrong with you anyways?"

"I guess it's dis cold weather," Jackal said with a shiver. "It's freezing my brain."

"Well, you better warm it up!" Reggie

 76

warned. "We've gots a lot of work to do, and I need you alert and focused, okay?"

"Sure, Reg," Jackal sighed. "Let's just get dis over with, so we can get on home. I'm not feeling so good."

Reggie rolled his eyes and shuffled the others along. "Come on, Raven," he sneered. "Get in der. We haven't gots all day you know?"

Raven seemed more concerned with what the ice was doing to her nails than Reggie's forceful tone. She continually checked the red polish she had so carefully painted on, which was already becoming chipped and cracked. Just about ready to open her mouth and complain, she noticed Reggie staring back at her. Not in a mood to start up, she kept her mouth shut and entered the bar.

Smelly's Bar was always the same. Small, cold, and depressing. Perfect for a couple of miserable Alleys looking for something to do. Despite a few minor enhancements, the joint remained the same old, dark, dank, rotten hole of a place as it had ever been. In regards to those small changes, Smelly had set up a few new stools made from some old coffee cans he found in the garbage. He put out a few flowers, which were all dead of course, and he convinced Thumbs to play a couple new songs. Other than that, the place was the same. Even the same old crowd sat around at the same shabby, wooden tables. The ever-devoted lowlifes of cat society, drowning their day away in stale beer.

Chapter Seven

Over the years, the place had been getting more and more rundown. Still, this little hole in the wall was very much Smelly's baby, even though times were tough. The few loyal patrons he did have often weren't enough. Without consistent business, it was becoming increasingly harder to stay open. The recent ice storm only added to the unfortunate situation.

As it had always been, Smelly himself manned the bar, wiping the counter with an icky, dirty rag. "Can I get you fellas a drink?" he asked as he saw the familiar faces enter. Deep down inside, he felt his heart skip a beat. The Silent Five didn't come around too much anymore unless they wanted something. Smelly would soon find out his instincts were right.

"We aren't just *fellas* here, Smelly!" Reggie said with a snap to his voice. "There's a lady here."

Smelly tilted his head just a bit. "Oh, hey der Raven," he smiled. "Good to see you."

"Yeah, whatever, toots," Raven snarled as she hoisted herself onto one of the upside-down flowerpots. "Just get me a beer and make it quick! After a long morning with these bozos, I need something cold and smooth and now!"

"Well, I never like to keep a lady waiting," Smelly said coyly. "I like to think that..."

"Awe, shut up, wouldya?" Reggie growled. "Just get us a round and be done with it!"

Smelly turned his rotund body around. He could feel his throat begin to swell, and he even

 78

began to tear up. Most Alleys didn't know it, but Smelly was very sensitive.

"Comin' right up!" Smelly sniffled with his back still to the others. He filled up five cups of beer as quickly as he could. "Here you go, fellas, and uh... Miss." He flung his old rag over his shoulder and returned to his other customers.

The Silent Five wandered over to their favorite table in the shadows, the very table where Grim had actually enjoyed himself just a short time ago. A small sprinkling of other Alleys filled some of the other tables, looking as miserable and flat as the beer they were drinking. As always, Thumbs, the saxophone player, was busily playing his gloomy tunes at the very back corner. It was totally depressing.

"So, what's our plan?" Jackal finally asked once they were all settled in at the table. "Are we gonna make an announcement or what?"

Reggie leaned forward and stared at each member. "I'll tell you what we are gonna do, we're gonna insist dat dey start now! Send 'em to da theater now!"

Slim, who had been quiet until this moment, couldn't help but say something. "Reggie, is der some reason you's acting like Fidel all of da sudden?"

"What?" Reggie snarled. "What did you say?"

Everyone looked slowly at Slim. "Well, to tell you da truth, you've been acting kinda like a jerk lately. Like you's in charge or something. If

Bait was here, you'd have to listen to him…"

"Bait is an idiot!" Reggie cried, his temper rising. "I know it! You know it! Fidel knows it! Once we can all admit dat, I will be takin' over as Fidel's partner! Dat's da plan, got it?"

"Whatever you say, Reg," Slim added. Deep down he knew just where Reggie was headed. He had seen this before. There was always someone in Fidel's private brood who started to feel a little too confident, got a bit cocky around the others. It was only a matter of time before Reggie ended up like the last guy to pull this routine. One day he just disappeared. Grim eventually replaced him. No one has seen or heard from him since. It's like he never existed.

"I'm ready for another beer," Cheeseburger said with a stupid sort of smile on his face. He was oblivious to the squabble between Reggie and Slim. As long as he was putting something in his mouth, he was in his own little world. "Ya think Smelly has any snacks here today? I'm starved!"

"Come on, we don't have time for dis," Reggie snapped. "Dis isn't boys' night out. Let's get to work!"

"The sooner da better," Jackal agreed. "I just wanna get some shut eye."

Just then, Cheeseburger walked toward the bar.

"And just where is you going?" Reggie asked, eyeing Cheeseburger like a hawk.

"I, uh…, was gonna go see if Smelly had

some treats," Cheeseburger said with a little lift to his voice. "Ya know, like I said before."

"Get back here!" Reggie snapped. Slim was right. Reggie was acting just like Fidel. That's all anyone needed. Another Fidel. "Sit down! There's no time to eat!"

Cheeseburger cowered back over to his seat looking defeated and sad. *I just wanted a little snack,* he mouthed to himself. He put his paw to his tummy and felt it rumble.

"Listen fellas," Raven piped in, "let's get movin' already. I'm supposed to meet up with Fidel later. We're gonna…talk."

"Talk? Talk about what?" Jackel asked. "Fidel doesn't *talk* to anyone."

"Well he's gonna talk to me, you know, like a normal boyfriend."

"Boyfriend?" everyone suddenly piped in. "Boyfriend?"

"Haven't you two been down dis road before?" Jackel asked. "I don't think it's such a hot idea."

"Dis time is gonna be different," Raven went on. "I gotta a plan, see? I'm gonna tell Fidel dat it's my way or the…"

"Awe, shut up already!" Reggie blared. "Nobody cares, lady! This ain't no talk show! Now let's get back to business!"

There had never been a female in the Silent Five before. In fact, Reggie, Jackal and the rest of the gang didn't talk to females very much. Most of their acquaintances were males. Every so often, they spoke to the occasional female at the Glitterbox, but those girls were different.

For a moment, the Silent Five were silent, just as they were always supposed to be. Then, in a sudden move, Reggie leapt up on top of his stool. Looking over the meager crowd, he cleared his throat and began. "Listen up, everyone!" Smelly stared at him with a combination of fear and confusion. This had all the ear markings of a sketchy situation. "I need every one of you's to come with us down to da Hope Street Theater! We's gonna set all you up as guards!"

"What about our beer?" Steak, one of the loyal customers, shouted out. Steak wasn't in Fidel's elite group of Alleys, but he had always been part of his revolving circle. Steak had actually fought beside Fidel on many occasions.

"I just ordered dis one!"

" Then you had better gulp it down fast!" Reggie went on. "Like I said, you's all coming with us. Fidel's orders!"

Despite Reggie's threatening tone, no one was too sure about this plan. After all, they had never been forced to listen to him before.

"Where's Bait?" Fink, another patron, shouted. "Why ain't he tellin' us all dis? Why's you here?"

"Because I am!" Reggie roared. "You got a problem with dat, you can go discuss it with Fidel!" He rubbed a bead of sweat from his forehead and took in a quick and deep breath. "So who's ready?"

Life Eight

"I'll go!" Smelly volunteered, his paw raised proudly in the air.

Reggie took one look at his round body. "Sorry pal, you're just not right for the job. You better man da bar, Smells. It's what you oughta do."

Smelly crumpled his old rag in his paws. He felt a familiar swell in his throat and a moistness in his eyes. "Awe, dat's okay," he said as convincingly as he could. "I gots too much to do anyway. Da people will be having a party upstairs tonight, and I need to be fetching some more beer."

Reggie nodded and looked back over at all the tables. "Well?" he called. "Anyone out there?" Sitting near the back, an Alley named Mustard called out from the darkness. "What's at the Hope Street Theater anyway? Why do we's got to go there, huh? It's cold outside, and I've got other plans."

In a growing rage, Reggie stood up tall on all fours, knocking his stool upside down. In slow Fidel-like steps he pranced over to Mustard, swatting at every beer mug he passed. The stale, warm liquid flew up and into all the jaw-drooped faces, stinging and burning their eyes. Finally, he reached Mustard, leaned in toward his raggedy face, and hollered, "I said, you're coming with me! Now get off your paws and let's go!"

Mustard seemed to shrink under the table. He had never seen Reggie act like this. The Silent Five had always been so...silent. It was clear Reggie was losing it. There's only so much pressure a leading Alley can take before he ultimately starts to crack up. It happened time and time again.

Chapter Seven

By this time, Slim, Jackal, Cheeseburger, and Raven had all sucked down the last of their beers. Fearful for what Reggie might say or do, they lined up by the front entrance, waiting for further instructions. Jackal stood there, shaking his head in disapproval. He didn't like this Reggie.

One by one, the rest of the Alleys got to their feet. There were only twelve of them. They nodded to Smelly as they passed him by, and met with the rest of the Silent Five near the front. They were ready to go to the theater.

Nobody spoke after that. Nobody knew why they were going to this theater, let alone where the theater even was. Instructions would come later. That was the usual way of the Alleys. Listen, don't argue, and follow orders. They knew the drill all too well.

With a single nod, Reggie led the gang on the icy hike to their next stop; the Glitterbox. He puffed the cold air from his body and watched it disappear. "Let's go!" he roared. "There's no time to lose! We've got a job to do!" Like obedient, little ants, they all followed on the dirty, icy streets. Two steps behind, Raven checked her nails again. They were all chipped.

 84

Chapter Eight

The Hope Street Theater sat quiet and still. Candle wandered around the big, empty building waiting for someone to arrive. Just when she was about to give up and head to her room for a nap, Fluffy wandered in. Candle could hear him at the front entrance. She knew right away it was him. She recognized his scent.

"Hi, Fluff," Candle said shyly, watching the big, white cat walk through the lobby of the once great theater. "You're here early," she smiled.

"It's not *that* early," Fluffy teased. He watched the little tuft of red fur atop Candle's head sway gently to one side. "It's almost noon, you know?"

"Noon? Is it really?" Candle asked. "My goodness, I could've sworn it was much earlier." She took a moment to glance around the room. "I guess time goes by slowly when you're all alone in a place like this."

"Well, maybe I could spend a little more time here, if you don't mind," Fluffy said, a strong look in his eye. "I promise to behave this time."

Feeling a little flustered, Candle opened her mouth to answer when Mr. Shadow came bounding into the lobby. She felt a wave of relief.

"Mr. Shadow, good to see you," Fluffy said with a smirk toward Candle as the Stick School professor sauntered in. "Is that a new sweater you're wearing?"

Mr. Shadow, who had been wearing the same yellow sweater for as long as he could remember, glanced down at the torn garment. "Are you joking, son?" he snarled, his eyebrows all twisted together. "You must want something, is that it? Huh, *huh*?"

"No, no, of course not," Fluffy said. "I guess in the light it looked new, that's all. Promise."
Shadow pursed his lips and stared Fluffy down.

"I don't know, Fluffy," he began as he started to slowly walk away. "You're an odd one."

Fluffy watched as Shadow left the lobby and strolled into the main theater. A small bead of sweat bubbled under his fur. Candle giggled to herself. Like Shadow, she too figured Fluffy was up to something.

After a few moments, several other Sticks arrived. Tabitha, Snickers, Darla, and Twinkle Toes, just to name a few. They looked forward to getting together every day, just as they always had.

Life Eight

Having had a place like The Factory and now the theater was very important to their livelihood. In spite of all their hardships, they always had each other. No one could ever take that away.

After the usual morning hellos, everyone took a very welcomed seat. They were quite drained from the slippery walk over to the theater. It seemed walking on ice was not getting any easier.

While the ice storm was long over, the cold temperatures kept the ice solid. It wasn't just the cats who were dealing it. Several traffic accidents had already been reported as a result of the hazardous road conditions. There was no telling what would happen next. The best place for the Sticks, and all animals and people for that matter, was inside. For the Sticks, the Hope Street Theater was their haven away from home. At least there they'd be safe.

"Hi Darla," Candle called, flagging her girlfriend over. "How's the weather out there? Still cold?"

"Sorry, Candle," Darla whined, locking her back legs together. "But I gotta go to the litterbox. I'll catch up with you later!" Having a conversation with Darla was getting harder and harder. Her chronic bladder problems were becoming more and more of an inconvenience. It seemed she was always rushing off to use the box. In fact, there was even talk of getting Darla her own litterbox. Privacy.

After a few more minutes passed, Mr. Sox

entered the theater. Everything seemed to stop whenever he walked into a room. His endless knowledge, grace, and dignity had a power to it even he didn't quite understand. The respect he commanded was natural. No cat before or after would ever hold a candle to him. He was one of a kind.

Fluffy too saw Mr. Sox enter. He hadn't spoken to him since their recent argument. When Sox suggested they keep Fidel locked up in a makeshift cell in the basement of the theater, Fluffy was outraged. "Let's kill him!" Fluffy insisted. Sox wouldn't have it. The Sticks never were and never would be violent. Only in the heat of battle to defend themselves would they ever consider using force. Since Fidel's escape, the discussion had become moot. Still, the resentment lingered...on both sides.

"Hello, Mr. Sox," Fluffy said quickly. Like ripping off a Band-Aid, he knew he had to get this over with. The fact that Fluffy had lost a life since their last encounter might help somewhat to soften the blow. "Glad you could make it in today."

"Yes, yes of course," Sox mumbled in his direction with a hint of elderly attitude. It was clear he wasn't ready to rehash their fight. No doubt they would discuss it later. The air always had to be cleared where Mr. Sox was concerned. Unresolved issues were never allowed. For now, it would hover over them like a dead weight.

Shadow innocently walked by. "Mr. Sox,

Life Eight

I'm glad you're here," he said cheerfully despite the obvious elephant in the room. He too witnessed the fight between Sox and Fluffy.

"We've got a lot to talk about. Where shall we sit?"

"Sit? I don't want to sit," Sox moaned. "I want you to gather all the Sticks and meet me on the stage. It's time we get back to business." His frail, little body headed into the theater. Shadow watched him struggle to the stage, when a sudden and disturbing thought came to him. *When Sox is gone, will I take over as the Stick leader?* Feeling silly and somewhat guilty, he rattled his head back and forth, knocking the notion right out of it.

"Listen up, everyone!" Shadow called. His voice bounced off the high lobby ceiling. "Meet on the stage in two minutes! Two minutes! Sox has an important meeting scheduled! And I said *important!*"

Until Shadow mentioned Sox's name, nobody budged. As much as they all respected Shadow for his wisdom and experience, there was something satisfying about ignoring him. But once the name of their fearless leader spewed from his mouth, they all sprang into action.

Sox stood on the stage and waited. In his right paw, he held tightly to a wooden cane, which was actually a toy cane he had found from some sort of weird old man doll. What kid would want that?

For Sox, it was becoming increasingly

89

difficult to just stand sometimes. His body seemed to be growing a little bit weaker with each passing day. Never one to complain, he held onto his cane. He was far too proud to ever let on he was having any trouble. He knew the last thing anyone needed to worry about was his wellbeing.

"What's this about, Sox?" Waffles asked as he headed up the stage stairs.

Behind Waffles, Uncle Fred teetered along. "Yeah, Mr. Sox," he said, bits of leaves stuck to the top of his head. "What's the meeting about? Do you have a big announcement or something?"

"Let's just wait for everyone else, my son," Sox said calmly. "I want everyone here first."

After a few moments, everyone had made their way to the stage. Sox stood dead center, while the others formed a circle around him. Draped behind them all was the theater's grand, old curtain. Ripped and worn from years of neglect, just the sight of it reminded everyone of what would have been a glorious night at the theater.

Fluffy and Mr. Shadow glanced up at the sound booth, looking for Ned, the angry ghost of the theater, the very ghost that pushed Grim to his seventh death, not that anyone else knew that. Fluffy and Shadow exchanged looks of worry, then quickly turned away from the booth. It was better not to look.

"Why don't you have a seat, Mr. Sox?" Waffles asked politely. Sox leaned against his cane and looked somewhat uncomfortable.

Life Eight

"We could all sit too? We don't mind, do we fellas?"

The rest of the gang nodded, as Sox blurted, "No! I will not sit! I will remain standing."

Waffles and the others slowly stood back up. They gave each other quick reassuring glances that Sox was, in fact, okay.

"I called you all in here today," Sox began, as powerful as ever, "so we could discuss our continued renovation of the theater." Despite his earlier outburst, Sox sat down. The others followed his lead, not questioning why, not even with their eyes.

"Well, I've been cleaning up a little since the fight," Candle said in reference to the battle between the Sticks, Alleys, and the newly formed Troop members. "There really wasn't much to be done. Just some upside down chairs, that sort of thing." Her eyes wandered over to another part of the stage. "Oh, and just a little bit of blood." Candle looked over at Fluffy with a crooked smile. The blood on the stage was his.

"Good, very good, Candle," Sox went on. "We can always count on you to help. I appreciate all you've done."

"Sure, but it really was nothing," Candle blushed. This time, Fluffy smiled in her direction.

"Of course. So, going on, Mr. Shadow," Sox continued, "I'd like you to be in charge of setting up the new Stick School. You know everything we need to do, and for that I think you'll be the best man for the job."

Chapter Eight

"Thank you, sir," Shadow affirmed. "Glad to be of service."

"Any thoughts on where the school will be located?"

"Oh, yes," Shadow charmed. "If you take a look just past stage left, you'll notice a small door just beyond the exit." Shadow stepped ever closer, coming dangerously near the edge of the stage. "Behind that door is an old rehearsal room where..." Suddenly, Mr. Shadow lost his footing and slipped off the stage, landing flat on his bottom.

Everyone rushed over. "Are you all right?" Tabitha cried. She had been so instrumental in helping Shadow when he fell on the island, that even something like a little stage fall sent her running. "How are your legs? Can you move?" She bent over the stage with the others surrounding her.

Shadow opened his eyes and gave her the thumbs up. "I'm all right, everyone," he said, his insides burning with embarrassment. "Nothing to see here," he added, struggling to get up in a pile of old music stands. "Go back to the meeting. I'll be right there."

Mr. Shadow had fallen right into the big, empty orchestra pit where all the beautiful music once came. The pit was one of the theater's most cherished attractions. Very modern for its day, it had all the newest bells and whistles. It was an honor to perform in the *pit*, as they called it. Musicians from all around the world were invited

Life Eight

Chapter Eight

to play in the orchestra. Now many years later, it looked like a pile of garbage. Twisted, black metal music stands, ripped sheet music, and broken chairs filled the deep hole. Another sad reminder of what once was.

"In that case, let us continue," Mr. Sox said as he casually repositioned his wire glasses. He was nearly blind without them. He flattened out some of his silver fur with his paw. "Shadow will be in charge of the Stick School. Candle, you will continue working in the dressing rooms. Every room in this theater is useful to us. Let me know who will be on your team."

"Sure, Mr. Sox," Candle said. She had been so busy fixing up her own room, she didn't know when she'd have the time to work on the others. "We'll get everything in shape before you know it."

"Great."

Mr. Shadow had finally managed to get back up onto the stage. After his little slip, only his ego was bruised, nothing else. "Okay, Mr. Sox," he began, rubbing his front paws together, "I think we all know what to do, so why don't we get back to work. Everyone, resume your same positions as before. Let me know if anyone needs any help."

Shadow turned to walk away when Fluffy suddenly opened his big mouth and yelled, "Aren't we forgetting something?" the mood in the room suddenly grew very tense.

"What's that, son?" Mr. Sox asked,

quickly reminded of their recent argument, praying this would not lead to another. "What are we forgetting?"

"Aren't we going to talk about Fidel? Aren't we going to figure out what to do about him?"

"What's to say?" Sox added with that wise look he often got in his eye when he wants someone to answer their own question.

"What's to say? Are you serious?"

Mr. Sox took small, slow steps over to Fluffy. He lowered his glasses, as Fluffy was now close enough to see, and took in a long, deep breath. "Fluffy, you and I have shared some words lately, and let's just say, I hope we have none today." Sox sat down, still clutching his cane. "I know Fidel is out there, and no, I'm not trying to avoid it. He's alive and as big a threat to us Sticks as ever, maybe even more."

"Yeah, and...?" Fluffy snapped.

"There's something I want you to understand, Fluffy," Mr. Sox continued. Everyone else on the stage had now moved closer, anxious to hear what Sox would say next. "Many of you have spent all your lives living in fear of Fidel. Day and night, everything has always been about Fidel. Your lives have revolved around that anguish. It has consumed us."

Sox paused, swallowed hard, and then went on. "That is not living. Not the kind of living the great Bubastis would hope for us. Not the kind of living I would wish on any of you. I think it's time we live our lives for ourselves. Now, don't get me wrong, he's out there, just like always. That in itself makes me angry, very angry!" Sox yelled. He paused a moment, composed himself, and then continued. "So yes, we will station guards around the theater, we will always be on the lookout, and we must resume combat training classes once Mr. Shadow reopens Stick School, but at the same time, Fidel doesn't have to control our lives, not if we don't let him. Don't you think it's time we all deserve that?"

Mr. Sox sat back and waited. Fluffy didn't make a fuss. Not this time. He glanced over at Candle who looked as though she was on the edge of her seat, awaiting an awful scene. To her delight, Fluffy calmly nodded in Sox's direction.

"Well put, Mr. Sox," Shadow said. "And let me just add that I totally agree. We don't need to spend all our time thinking about Fidel. You said it so well, so magnificently, that I..."

"Oh, stop kissing up," Mr. Sox said, completely out of character. "I already put you in charge of Stick School. There's no reason to press your luck."

"Sorry, sir, I mean, Mr. Sox," Shadow mumbled.

"So, unless anyone else has anything more to say?" Sox went on, anticipating some response. No one spoke up. "Very well, let's get back to work. I'll be here for a little while longer, then I must be going home. You'll forgive me, but I'm

Life Eight

awfully tired."

"Why don't you rest here?" Tabitha suggested. "There's plenty of places where you can relax." She smiled politely at her leader with genuine concern. She had always had a huge heart.

Sox rubbed his eyes with the back of his paw. "Thank you, Tabitha, but no," he sighed. "I'd like to rest on my own pillow, if you don't mind, but I thank you dearly for the suggestion."

"Sure, Mr. Sox," Tabitha said. "I understand."

After a while, he left, just like he said he would.

Chapter Nine

On the other side of town, The Silent Five had just entered the Glitterbox. While they had managed to recruit several Alley guards at Smelly's Bar, they hadn't gathered enough. Besides, the crowd at the Glitterbox was more promising. They were more energetic than the sluggish, lowlifes often found at Smelly's. So, while the group from Smelly's was forced to wait outside in the cold, the others ventured in. Right away, Reggie spotted Bait in the back corner.

"Bait, what are you doing here?" Reggie asked as he entered through a wall of purple streamers. "How long've you been here?"

Bait sucked down his beer then turned to face Reggie. "I'm workin', what do you tink I'm doing?" Then he burped.

Reggie looked at all the empties on the

 98

table. "It don't look like you's working to me, Bait."

"Well, I am, so why don't you just leave me alone," Bait mumbled, turning his back to Reggie.

Reggie could feel the fire in his belly ignite. He rolled his eyes and snarled under his breath. He hated Bait. Sooner or later, he'd burst. "Come on, gang," Reggie said to the others. "There's a table over der. Let's sit and get a drink before we makes our announcement."

The other four looked back and forth between Bait and Reggie. They hesitated, not really sure which table to sit at. Reggie, of course, expected everyone to follow him. After all, he had taken it upon himself to be in charge of the group. Naturally, they should sit at his table.

On the other hand, Bait was Fidel's right hand man, the closest link to Fidel. As demanding as Reggie was, Bait was the one they needed to follow. This was their job, after all. For Reggie, like it or not, he needed to realize he was just one of the gang.

Slim, Jackal, Cheeseburger, and Raven all sat with Bait, making it a point not to look at Reggie. They knew better. He was scowling in their direction.

Reggie sat alone at a small table, bubbling with a growing anger. The longer he sat there, the more he could feel a tight knot welling deep inside of him. A few more minutes passed, and he couldn't take it any longer. Sucking in his pride, he stood up, flipped his stool, stomped over to Bait's table, and begrudgingly sat down. He knew he had been beaten, but sitting alone was not going to impress

Chapter Nine

Fidel. They all had a job to do, and getting it done was priority. Sulking wasn't going to cut it.

After a few moments, one of the waitresses came by to take their orders. It wasn't difficult. There was only one item on the menu…beer. Flat and stale, of course.

"Beers for everyone, toots," Bait said. "Make it quick, got it?"

"Sure thing," the waitress said. "Six brews, comin' right up! Be back in a snap!" The waitress was a small, pretty cat, the kind one sees in magazines and on commercials. She was much too pretty to be working in a dive like the Glitterbox. Yet times were tough, as they always had been, and a job's a job. As she walked away, Bait and the other males watched her bottom as it wiggled away.

Raven curled her lip and cracked, "Well, she's a snobby little thing, ain't she? I can't stand dames like dat."

"Awe, you're just jealous, Raven, dat's all," Jackal teased.

"Jealous?" Raven cried. "Why would I be jealous of her?"

"Oh, never mind." Jackal and the others stared wide-eyed as the waitress returned. She held the tray of beers high over her head without even so much as a wobble in her step. In no time, she had placed all the drinks on the table.

"Der you go, fellas," she said. "Enjoy."

"Fellas? Who you callin' a fella?" Raven snarled, rising to her feet with a low hiss and probing stare.

"Sor-ry, ma'am," the waitress apologized. "I guess I didn't see you sittin' there."

"Ma'am? *Ma'am?*" Raven scowled. "I'll show you who's a ma'am..."

"Sit down and shut up, Raven!" growled Reggie. "You're embarrassing all of us! This is not how the Silent Five behave, and I won't have it!"

Raven couldn't believe what she was hearing. "You serious?" she cried. "Who made you the model of good behavior, eh?" She leaned in close to Reggie's face. They were not an inch apart.

"Awe, shut it, will you?" Bait wailed as he slammed his mug down on the table. "Da both of you's is gonna be fired if you don't stop it! Now sit down and let's figure out what's we gotta do here, all right?"

"I'll sit down if she sits down!" Reggie whined, still nose to nose with Raven.

Raven sat first, though she never allowed the scowl on her face to fade. Like it or not, she was stuck with Reggie. While some jobs have their perks, this job, unfortunately, had him.

"Good, dat's real good," Bait said calmly once everyone was seated. "Now, if you don't mind, I'm gonna tell everybody here what dey gots to do about da theater and stuff."

"Well, if *you* don't mind, Bait, I think maybe I should be da one to make da announcement," Reggie said, his foul attitude in full swing. "After all, I handled da crowd at Smelly's Bar quite well. Dey's all outside this bar waiting for my next instructions. So like I said, if *you* don't mind, I think I'll take over."

Keeping his position in mind, Bait ignored Reggie and leapt onto his chair. He cleared his musty, old throat, and with a sharp, whiny voice declared, "Listen up, all you's lowlifes!" The hustle and bustle of the club stopped. The music, the dancers, all of it. Bait had everyone's attention. "I need you all to come with us. It seems 'dos Sticks is up to no good!"

"Awe, dey's always up to no good," someone from the crowd shouted. "Just leave 'em be. Who cares?"

"Maybe you don't all know it, but Fidel was chained up, see, by those Sticks, and we gotta get 'em!" Bait roared on. "He's da one who sent me here, so we's all gotta listen!"

"We know all about Fidel at that theater," another voice called from the crowd. "What's Fidel want us to do about it anyway?"

Feeling powerful, Bait leaned down and picked up his beer. He took a hearty swig followed by a loud burp. Once he was done wiping the froth from his jaw with the side of his arm, he opened his mouth and shouted, "We are going to dat theater to keep 'dos Sticks in der place! We's gonna surround dat theater and not let dem out! Ever!"

"Well, what's dat gonna do?" Max, the club's owner, shouted.

"Yeah, we just gonna stand around da theater waitin' or something?" someone else piped in.

"No, you guy's ain't gettin' it!" Bait roared. "We's not gonna just stand around, we's gonna..."

"What Bait is *trying* to say," Reggie interrupted as he too stood up on his chair, looking out over the crowd with a sudden sense of control, "is, we are going to the theater to make sure 'dos Sticks don't get out. We're gonna starve dem, and keep dem captive right der in their own stupid little Stick world, got it?"

Bait scooted over as much as he could without falling. There was no way he was going to share the limelight with a sour puss like Reggie.

Max stepped out of the crowd and stood right before Bait and Reggie. "What about all da Sticks dat are at home, you know, their people's home?" he asked Bait. He turned to Reggie and continued with, "And don't you think da Sticks can find a way out? I hate to say it, but 'dos Sticks is smart."

"But we're smarter!" Reggie said sternly, eyeing everyone in the place. He leaned as far away from Bait as he could without falling. Until he stood next to him, he didn't realize how much Bait actually smelled. "Most of da Sticks is at dat theater during the day doing their stupid little Stick stuff with their stupid little Stick feet. The good ones for sure, you know, da main guys will be there. You can mark my words."

Finally, Bait and Reggie managed to get the crowd on their side. It didn't take much to woo the Alleys into action. Anything involving battle-mode got their attention, especially where the Sticks were concerned. While most of them would have preferred to sit at the club all day and night, the prospect of fighting the Sticks was always enticing. They were Alleys, after all, fighting cats.

Everyone was on their way, when Max made a desperate plea. "Come on, fellas," he began, thinking only of his business. "Stay a while! The drinks is on me!" Glancing over at the stage, he had another idea. "The...the show is about to start! Our best dancing girls will be on that stage in no time! Trust me, you don't wanna miss it!"

All the Alleys turned to Bait, hoping for an answer to their dilemma. Bait stood there, imagining all those dancing girls, free drinks, and of course, more dancing girls.

"Awe, come on males!" Bait shouted. "You can hang here anytime! Dis is important stuff we's doing! Besides, it's what we gotta do!"

"We're with you, Bait!" someone called out.

"Yeah, just lead da way!" cried a guy with a pink feather boa wrapped around his neck. "We'll follow you, Bait!"

Surprised by the crowd's sudden enthusiasm, Bait leapt off the table with a huge grin. He waved his arm overhead yelling, "Dis way, fellas! Follow me to da theater!"

Reggie too jumped down. Having no choice but to let Bait take charge, he begrudgingly stood beside him as the Alleys poured toward them.

Life Eight

"Let's go to da theater!" Bait roared.

As Bait led everyone out, Max gave it one more try. "Don't leave! I got free drinks and fresh fishies on da way!"

"Awe, he's bluffin'," Bait said. "He ain't got no fish. Refocus males, and follow me!"

Max rushed over to his stage and flipped on the music. "Start dancing! Start dancing!" he cried to the girls. "Come on, Bait's gonna put me out of business if you don't start movin'!" Max threw pawfuls of feathers and glitter on the girls as if that would somehow entice the others to stay. He ran from girl to girl, lifting their arms, pushing their hips back and forth, whatever he could do to get them moving. Despite his frantic efforts, the girls just stood there, paws on their hips, as they watched the crowd leave.

"Give it up, Max," Claudia said as she removed a blue feather from her ear. "There's no use. Look, they's all left."

Max turned to the door and saw it was true. Every last Glitterbox patron was gone. All that remained was a bunch of upside-down tables, broken beer mugs, and feathers. The dancing girls stood on the stage looking dumbfounded.

"Get outta here!" Max snarled at them. Without customers, what did he need entertainment for? "What's da use? Just get out!"

One by one, the females filed off the stage. They ran into their meager little dressing room, grabbing what was left of their feathers, hats, and other costume pieces, and charged out the

Chapter Nine

entrance. All alone in the silence, Max sat at the center table, put his head in his lap, and cried. The only one who saw him was Spencer, a small, baby mouse left behind by his family. With any luck, he'd grow up to be a traveling mouse and leave this rotten city behind.

Chapter Ten

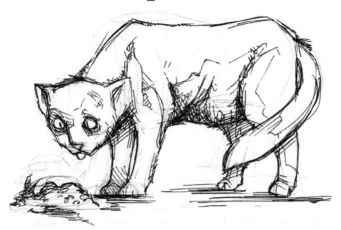

Grim watched Terrence carefully as he prepared what would become their dinner. Finding edible food at Maxi's house was like finding a needle in a haystack. Not only did Maxi almost never feed her cats, but for the very few times she did, it was always some sort of rotten, stale, molded cat food that would surely end all nine lives of whoever dared eat it. Needless to say, Terrence and the others had gotten very accustomed to finding their own food, much like other Alley cats.

"Here, want some of this?" Terrence asked Grim, holding a glob of something gooey.

"What is…that?" Grim asked, ogling the stuff like it was some sort of poisoned mush. "Looks nasty."

Terrence gave it a lick. "Naw, it's good."

Chapter Ten

"All right, I'll give it a try," Grim finally said, feeling his stomach turn in knots. "But only because I'm really hungry."

Not taking his grimacing eyes from Terrence, Grim brought the goo to his quivering mouth. Sticking out his rough, pink tongue he took one tiny taste. Terrence waited anxiously for his reaction. In another world, Terrence would have wanted to be a chef.

"Yuck! Gross!" Grim cried, his face looking like he had just bitten into a lemon. He shook the remaining sludge from his paw and spit out what he could. "That's awful! What is it?"

"I call it *road kill mash*," Terrence proudly said. "It's taken me a little while to perfect, but I think I've got it down pretty good."

"Road kill mash?" Grim wallowed in horror. "Are you joking? You trying to kill me or something?"

"Awe, it's not that bad, Grim," Terrence teased, "especially when I get the good stuff."

"Good stuff? What's the good stuff?"

"Squirrel mostly. Not many of those around here, though," Terrence explained. He was enjoying watching Grim squirm at the details. "This was mostly rabbit guts with a little dash of worm paste."

"Are you serious?" Grim screeched. "You eat that stuff? I'm not a lion, you know, I'm a *domestic* cat! I don't eat road kill!"

"Suit yourself," Terrence smiled, scooping

another pile into his mouth. "More for me."

Grim watched in horror as Terrence ate more and more of the nasty delicacy. It was gross. "So, I'm going to head back to the hospital," he said, trying to distract himself from the nasty food. "Tonight's the night I'm gonna find my way in. You know, search for Dennis." He paused and let his stomach growl itself into a frenzy. "I'll find something to eat along the way. I'll check the alleyways for some real food."

"Very funny, Grim," Terrence teased. "Just don't get your hopes up, you know?"

"What do you mean by that?"

"Well, with Dennis," Terrence said somberly. "I don't want you to get upset. Don't forget to be realistic, that's all."

Grim scrunched his eyebrows together. He glared at Terrence with angry eyes. "I know about being realistic," he snarled. "You don't need to remind me."

Terrence stepped back. "Sorry, pal, I was just trying to help, that's all." He really didn't mean to offend Grim, just give him some good old fashioned advise.

"Yeah, whatever," Grim sighed, staring up into the darkening sky. "I'll see you later. Tell Miles not to wait up for me. I'll find him in the morning."

"Sure thing, Grim," Terrence said. "Be careful out there."

Grim scowled once more in Terrence's

direction. He didn't like it when others got all preachy on him. It made him feel like a child. After another moment, Grim finally walked away, heading right for the hospital. Terrence watched with a nervous stomach as Grim disappeared into the night. He didn't have a good feeling about this, not in the least.

Chapter Eleven

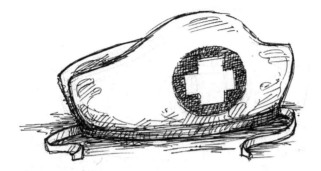

Grim managed to find himself a decent dinner. Luckily, there was an old burger stand near the hospital. It was just a small, wooden shack, but it was perfect to a cold, hungry cat. Taking a chance, Grim rushed behind it when the chef wasn't looking. Sure enough...gold.

At the top of a large trashcan above an endless pile of junk, sat several burnt patties. Charred or not, they smelled delicious and tasted even better. Nothing fancy, but far better than Terrence's homemade concoction of mangled mashed-up mush. Anything was better than that. Anything.

Once his belly was full and he had made the trek over to the hospital, Grim soon found himself patrolling the floors. Sneaking in turned out to be far easier than he had expected. Once through a small, broken window he had seen during his stake out, he was home free.

Getting around unseen was easy as well. The hospital had a multitude of passageways, empty halls, and patients either too sick or too blind to bother.

By way of stairwells and air ducts, Grim made his way up to the floor where he believed Dennis to be. His old Stick School training was paying off once again.

Quickly but quietly, Grim hopped down from a ceiling vent, landing himself on a grey carpeted hallway. The carpet looked and smelled old, like it hadn't been changed or cleaned in years. The walls were a boring pale peach color, and the fluorescent lighting from above was actually painful to look at. All in all, everything was quite ugly.

Keeping a keen eye out for danger, Grim quickly spotted a good hiding spot. It was a hospital bed just sitting in the hall. He dashed under it. A sick, old lady trying to get some sleep lay above him. The sounds of her snoring were loud, rough, and terribly annoying. The lady was hooked up to all kinds of wires and tubes and too doped up to notice an insignificant little cat lurking under the wheels. Taking a leap of faith, Grim stepped out to search for what would most likely be Dennis's room.

Slinking down the hall, Grim could hear a lot of activity up ahead. Being so late at night, he figured that was unusual, even for a hospital.

Life Eight

Tip-toing as much as one with large, pointy claws can, he inched his way toward the noise. As he grew closer, he could hear people talking, but he was still too far away to make out what they were saying.

A bit further up the hall, Grim came to a sort of fork in the road where it split off into three different directions. A very large, round desk sat right at the center of all three corridors. The desk was big enough to seat at least ten people. Stacks of papers, coffee mugs, and an endless supply of hard candy lay scattered across the top. Quite a few nurses in big, stiff white hats mulled around filing their nails and chomping ferociously on flavorless gum. They were the ones he had heard talking.

Maybe it's over there, thought Grim, trying hard to imagine where the camera flashes had come from. Very carefully, he continued on, keeping a close watch on the nurses. To his great fortune, they were far too preoccupied with themselves to notice the likes of him.

Keeping close to the wall, Grim walked on as inconspicuously as he could. With his head down and his tail tucked under his belly, he felt confident he was heading in the right direction.

On Grim's left were a series of patient rooms. For most of them, the doors were open. He peeked into each room as he passed, trying to see beyond the long curtain that hung as a source of privacy for the sick people unfortunate enough to be there.

Chapter Eleven

The foul smell of hospital food lingered in the air. Dishes like liver and onions, pot roast, and cabbage soup should only be made by experienced professionals, not cafeteria employees. No disrespect. To keep from getting too queasy, Grim breathed through his mouth, a habit he normally hated in others.

Grim soon found himself at another crossroads. Staring at another fork, he paused and mentally debated the different options. The two hallways before him split off in opposite directions. They looked exactly the same. Dark, lonely, sad. With nothing to lose, Grim was about to give the left a shot, when he overheard an interesting conversation. He stood as stiffly as he could and listened.

"Those boys have got to go," a female voice said in a snotty tone. "They're driving me crazy! They just want! Want! Want!"

"Give the guys a break, Flo," another deep but female voice answered. "They were hit by ice, for heaven's sake. Do you realize how much that must've hurt? Besides, one of them is dead. You should just be nice."

The word *dead* alerted all of Grim's senses. He heard the news reporter say one of the boys was dead at the scene, but was this nurse talking about the same boy? Did someone else die right here in the hospital? Was it Dennis? Grim had to know, and he had to know fast. His heart started to race, and his body began to sweat. Clenching his paws into tight balls, he waited for the nurses to continue, praying they'd say Dennis was alive.

"Well, Claudia," said Flo, the first nurse to speak. "They are very spoiled boys. You know the type, always getting what they want."

"I don't know," Claudia went on. "That one kid is really sweet, you know? He's a real good kid. Real good."

Who are you talking about? Grim shouted in his head. *Say it! Just say it so I know!*

"Oh, you mean that Dennis kid?" Flo finally asked.

"Yeah, Dennis."

Grim's fur stood straight up, and his ears pointed directly at the sky.

"Yeah, he's okay, I guess," Flo said. "I guess he's been real nice, but he's the only one," she added with a sharp wave of her finger. "Those other two must've gotten hit really hard in the head with that ice. Really hard."

"Well, they're just kids," Claudia added. "At least the cameras went home."

"Oh, they'll be back tomorrow," Flo teased. "Mark my words, honey. Room C23 will be in the hot seat for a long time."

Room C23! That must be the place! Grim thought to himself. Taking a quick glance around, he searched for something that would lead him in the right direction, the direction of C23. After a brief moment, he found exactly what he was looking for.

Right above Grim's head was a sign that read: *Patient Rooms C1-12* and beside it was

Chapter Eleven

another reading: *Patient Rooms C13-24.* Beside each sign was an arrow pointing one way or the other down the hall. C23 was to Grim's right, and that is exactly where was headed.

Grim checked carefully to make sure everything was clear. The hallway to his right looked as dark and quiet as the others. He searched for the nurses. They were going the other way. Making sure there was no one else watching him, Grim paused for just one more moment. If he were to be spotted, it would be the Pound for sure. Getting thrown into the Pound was not how he had planned on spending his evening.

Feeling confident in his obscurity, Grim headed down the hallway. The grey, stained carpet was rough and felt funny under his paws. As irritating as it was, it was still an improvement over walking the icy sidewalks.

The first room to the right was C13. Unfortunately, that meant that C23 was likely all the way at the end of the hall. As Grim crept along his way, imagining what he'd find when in Dennis's room, he kept a sharp eye out for anything suspicious. Though he saw nothing out of the ordinary, he did spot the clock. Visiting hours were over. The only people in the hospital were those who had to be there, and of course, him.

C14, C15, C16... Grim walked slowly and carefully. He was almost there. His anticipation was growing. Dennis was near, and he could feel it. C23 was in reach.

All the rooms were on his right. The patients must have all been asleep, for it was very quiet aside from the occasional ringing phone at the nurses' station or maybe some footsteps from the floor above.

At last, Grim could see the door marked C23. Just a few feet away, his heart started to pound faster and faster. To his good fortune, the door was open just enough.

Grim poked his nose into the doorway of C23. It was dark. He listened very carefully. At first he heard nothing, however, when he focused harder, he could hear a faint beeping sound. *Must be one of the machines*, he said to himself.

Stepping in a little more, Grim stuck his ears out as far as he could. It was then he heard one of the most beautiful sounds he had ever heard. Dennis snoring. *Dennis!* he cried to himself. *I'd know that wheeze anywhere!* It filled his heart to know that such an insignificant, innocent little noise had brought him such pleasure.

Feeling confident he was in the right place, Grim walked into the room. A shiver of anticipation shuttered throughout his body. This was it.

As he entered, Grim noticed there were two patients in the room. *That must be one of the friends*, he wondered. *One of the other boys.*

Grim stepped in deeper. The room was white. It was quite small but large enough for two standard sized hospital beds. Both beds were engulfed in a long, white curtain used to ensure a sense of privacy for each patient. Behind Grim and up nearly to the ceiling was a television mounted with some sort of hardware. It was turned off.

Aside from the beds, there were a few garbage can type things, probably for towels, syringes, that sort of medical stuff. There was a sink with drawings above it showing exactly how to wash one's hands as if the next person using it had no idea how to perform such a mundane task. The walls had some signs, like how to use the call button, etc... Basically, the room was pretty drab and boring. Not what one would call five stars, then again, this was a hospital.

Grim thought about closing the door to the room to give him that extra security, but he decided against it. Perhaps the door was required to remain open because there were children inside.

After a big gulp of worry, Grim approached the first bed. He knew it was there because he could see the wheels peeking below the curtain. Besides, he could hear all that snoring.

Sticking his face in, Grim looked up at the tall bed beside him. Being a small cat, he couldn't see who was on top. Taking a chance he leapt up, landing quietly right on the edge of the bed. Now he could see the form of a body under the sheet, but he couldn't tell if it was Dennis. The boy's body was turned in the opposite direction,

Life Eight

and even the snoring wasn't enough to give him away.

Grim took a step closer. His heart sunk. There were white bandages wrapped all around this guy's head, from the neck up. Following a tube that was stuck in his arm, Grim's eyes wandered all the way up a tall pole finally reaching a bag of what he assumed was some sort of medicine. It looked awful, and to make things worse, there was another needle attached to his other arm. Whoever this was, Dennis or otherwise, was in pretty bad shape.

Grim continued to look around. In addition to the bed and the disturbing looking tubes, there was a small table beside the bed with a large, mauve colored pitcher. Beside that was a photograph in a small wooden frame. Grim leaned forward, but he couldn't make it out. Squinting his eyes tightly, he hoped to recognize someone from the picture. Chances were, if Dennis or someone from his family was in that picture, then this was Dennis under the sheet.

Finally Grim was close enough to see the photo. No Dennis. There were, however, two grown-ups, most likely the other boy's parents. In the photo they were both wearing wet suits and standing next to a very large and very dead fish. Weird picture. *Can't be Dennis in that bed,* Grim concluded. *The Crumbs would never fish.*

As relieved as Grim was to know that Dennis was not suffering in all those bandages and tubes, he was quickly reminded that there was still another boy in the room. He heard the familiar snore once again and immediately turned his head toward the other bed. *Are you Dennis? My Dennis?* Grim wondered as he stared at the hanging curtain that divided the room. It had to be Dennis.

Grim quickly leapt off the first bed and hopped onto the other. Once again, he could see the shape of a body under the thin, white sheet. With slow, tiny steps, he walked up the body toward the boy's face.

Like the other boy, this one was also wearing bandages around his head, but only at the top. Where there were bandages, Grim assumed, there must have been a lot of pain. Grim had hoped Dennis was somehow spared, but if this was, in fact, Dennis, then he too had been hurt. With a hard swallow, Grim took one more step toward the boy's face. His heart stopped. Dennis.

Dennis was fast asleep. Grim stared at him for a long moment, never looking away. Even though he had grown into a teenager, he still had the face of a boy. His sweet little nose, rosy lips, and round cheeks hadn't changed a bit.

Seeing Dennis's head all wrapped up like a mummy was a painful sight to take in. What were those bandages for anyway? Looking closer, Grim could see a large bulge on the side of his head. A small spot of blood stained through some of the gauze, which turned Grim's stomach into knots.

Life Eight

Chapter Eleven

Dennis's familiar scent was intoxicating. Grim took it in as if it was freshly baked bread. Only in his deathly dream state in the fictitious Grimsville had he smelled that glorious smell, but then again, that really didn't count. It never really happened.

Being this close to Dennis had put Grim into a slight trance. Despite the unfortunate circumstances, he felt happy, actually happy. He knew Dennis would be okay, at least, that's what he hoped would happen. Obviously, the doctors were working their hardest to make sure Dennis had the best care possible. Surely his parents were insisting on every treatment in the book. *Awe, he'll probably be home in a few days*, Grim thought. *I bet these bandages and stuff are only a precaution.*

Grim noticed a large machine sitting next to Dennis. It was near the wall and had some wires that ran all the way to his body, much like the tubes. On its tall, metal frame was a square monitor. It almost looked like a television, only this would surely be the most boring television show ever. The screen was black aside from a bouncing red dot. It bounced up and down in a rhythmic pattern making jagged, little lines like the tops of triangles. Every time it did, there was a loud beep. Grim had no idea what it was for, but he did remember seeing something like it on a show he had once watched with Dennis. *Must be something medical.*

Feeling more and more relaxed, Grim

glanced around the room just in case he overlooked something or someone. Perhaps Mrs. Crumb was asleep in the extra chair? Maybe there was a nurse quietly monitoring both boys? But in the darkness of the room, Grim's feline vision could see no one. For the first time in forever, he was alone with Dennis. The other boy didn't count.

Grim could feel his eyes well up with tears. No matter how much time had passed, no matter how much he had gone through or how busy his lives had gotten, he would never be able to shake the feeling of loneliness he had felt ever since leaving Dennis so long ago. Getting the Sleepy Potion would forever be the hardest, saddest day of his lives.

The painful memories of that day inspired in him an idea. Grim nuzzled himself against Dennis, right in the crook of his neck. A perfect fit. With a gentle purr, Grim sunk his body into the bed and gently closed his eyes. The feel of Dennis's breath on his head was the most comforting feeling he could've ever imagined.

After a few minutes of pure bliss, Grim could feel Dennis start to move. He let out a slight groan and wiggled his body into a different position. Grim's heart stopped once again. Was Dennis waking up? The idea was terrifying, but it didn't take long to realize that Dennis was still fast asleep. His snoring continued even deeper than before. In a move that Grim wasn't expecting, Dennis lifted his sleepy arm to rub his nose, then let it rest, right down on him, cradling him like a doll.

Even though Dennis was asleep and unaware of what he had just done, he had never made Grim happier. Grim reached his paw out and grabbed Dennis's arm, pulling it closer to him. In that moment, he didn't care about the Alleys, the Sticks, the Troops. All he wanted was to stay right there forever. All he wanted was to hear Dennis call his name one more time. Romeo. He finally remembered what it felt like to be Romeo. And it felt good.

Chapter Twelve

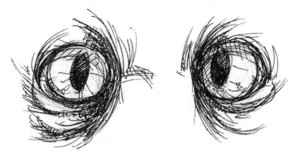

Early the following morning, the Silent Five made the treacherous journey over the ice all the way to the Hope Street Theater. By now some of the ice had melted leaving a grey, mushy slush to the already dilapidated state of the city. Trailing behind them were the reluctant recruits from Smelly's Bar and the Glitterbox.

By now, all the cats were tired, even the Silent Five, who were always expected to be in tip-top shape. Unfortunately, they had to spend much of the night torturing the recruits with endless babble about the plan. While everyone had to be present, it was Bait who did most of the talking.

"You'll stay at your posts and look for Sticks!" Bait told them a number of times. "Don't let 'em out of da theater, got it?"

Chapter Twelve

"We got it! We got it!" many of the recruits had said. "We know what to do. You've told us a million times! Don't let da Sticks out! Pretty simple stuff! Now, let us get some sleep, please!"

"There's no time for sleep!" Bait had cried during the never-ending training session. "Sleep is for wimps!"

"But we're tired!" the Alleys continued to plead as the night grew into morning. "How can we do anything without sleep?"

"Too bad!" Bait yelled at them, his own eyes becoming redder and more bloodshot by the second. No matter how hard he fought, his body was starting to droop, and his enthusiasm was crumbling. Whether he wanted to admit it or not, he also needed sleep.

Chapter Thirteen

Now that the threat of morning had become a reality and the sun was actually up, the time to strike had arrived. The tired Alleys sat like zombies across the street of the old theater. Bait still hadn't allowed them to sleep.

"Looks like a dump," Tuesday said when no one else had the energy to talk. "Who'd wanna live there?"

True, the theater wasn't as glorious as it once was, but a *dump*? That was debatable. Anyone with any sense of nostalgia could walk by the Hope Street Theater and imagine the beautiful building it had once been. They'd see past the rotted wood, the missing bricks, the faint glimmer of a marquee. Their vivid imaginations would once again have them staring at the flashy, vibrant theater that stood so long ago.

Chapter Thirteen

"Yep, pretty dumpy if you ask me," Delio agreed. "Looks like it's dead."

"Yeah, it's like a ghost," Tuesday added.

"Awe, who cares what da place looks like?" Bait snarled. "It's filled with Sticks, ain't it?" He paused just long enough to stretch his twisted body and yawn. "You fellas let me know how things turn out. I'll see you's back at da cave."

Bait turned to walk away when Reggie blared out, "Just where do you think you're going? You ain't leaving! You's da one dat brought us here in da first place!"

"Yeah! You cheating out on us?" sounded a voice from the crowd.

Cheatin' on you? I brought you here?" Bait cried, trying to sound innocent even in his complete guilt. He looked out at the fellas with his weary eyes and said, "Oh, all right, let's go get some shut-eye. But we don't have time to go back to da cave!"

"Thank goodness!" Raven roared. "If I don't get my beauty sleep, I end up lookin' like a mess!"

"You need more than beauty sleep, toots!" Bait snarked. Raven glared back with evil eyes.

Purposely ignoring Raven's probing stare, Bait searched around for a place to rest. "Everyone in dat alley over der!" he pointed in the direction of an alley across the street. "Find a spot and get some shut eye while you can! Remember, no funny business! I know where to find you if you try and skip out on me!"

Life Eight

Everybody waited until Bait was done with his rant. It usually took him between three and five minutes to tire himself out. His brain only had so much power.

When certain he was done spewing out orders, everyone rushed into that alley. In no time they were huddled under wet newspapers, old, ripped blankets, whatever they could find. It's amazing what one will put up with under extreme fatigue.

About two hours later, most of the Alleys started to awaken. One by one, they stretched themselves back on all fours and inched their way out of the alley. Leering at them from the entrance was Reggie, acting powerful and in charge. Bait on the other hand, was snoring away from the underside of a metal garbage can lid at the farthest end of the alley. He was all curled up like a little doll. It was pretty pathetic.

"Wake up!" Reggie shouted in Bait's direction.

Filled with annoyance, the others waited, still plenty tired themselves. Bait hadn't budged. He was a notoriously heavy sleeper. They all knew first hand how difficult it was to wake him up.

"Rise and shine!" Reggie shouted, this time right in Bait's crumpled ear. He grabbed a wooden spoon from the ground and banged it against the garbage can lid. "Get up, ya lazy bum!"

Bait shot up into the air like one of those old jack-in-the-box toys. His eyes burst open growing as wide as his gaping mouth. After about a five-foot drop, he landed on the lid. Because of the shape and slickness of it, the impact sent him soaring once again, this time straight across the alley. He finally plopped down just where he belonged, in a big pile of trash. "What's goin' on here?" he snapped, rotten banana peels hanging off his head. "What's da big idea?"

"Don't we need to get going?" Reggie snapped. "Isn't dat da plan? We can't just sleep all day, right?"

"How's about just a little more sleepy time first, eh?" Bait said with a hearty yawn. "Just long enough to.." Bait's voice trailed off as his eyelids grew heavier and heavier.

Filled with building rage, Reggie leapt forward, grabbed Bait by the neck, and yanked him up. "Sleep? Sleep?" he snarled, Bait dangling from his paw. "Aren't you da one who said there's no time for sleep?" Reggie threw Bait down and turned to the others. "Come on, fellas, let's get over to dat theater. Da Sticks'll be showing up soon. We wanna be there to make sure they stay." With a wicked grin, he marched off leaving Bait to marinate in the trash.

The Hope Street Theater was just across the street. Standing on the sidewalk, all the Alleys present for this little venture stared once again at the old building. It looked just as crummy now as it did two hours ago.

"So what do we do now, Reg?" Raven asked as she refluffed her unfluffed fur. "We gonna get dis show on da road or what?"

Life Eight

"This *show* is very important!" Reggie cracked. "Just follow me over der and we'll get set up just like we planned."

Feeling pushed aside, Bait charged forward. "Tanks, Reg, but I'll take it from here," he growled, stepping to the front of the line.

Reggie rolled his eyes, but he was smart. He knew that as much as he hated Bait and as much as he wanted to be the leader, Fidel had put Bait in charge. If he ever hoped on becoming Fidel's right hand man, he'd have to put his own intentions aside and follow orders. More than anything, that is what Fidel noticed. Conflict was never the road to impress Fidel. Respect was the only way.

"Okay, so it's late morning," Bait began as he stared up into the sky. "Da theater is right der," he pointed. "Remember your stations. Am I clear?"

Everyone looked at each other for answers. Either their own lack of sleep was contributing to their forgetfulness, or Bait had never given them specifics. In all that babble all night, he never once mentioned assigned stations.

"What are those stations again, Bait?" Reggie asked with a hint of cynicism. "I think some of us might have forgotten."

"Forgot? Whataya mean, you forgot?" Bait snarled in his high-pitched, annoying little voice. "You can't forget! You need to remember every last word I say, got it?"

"You never gave us no stations!" a voice called out.

131

Chapter Thirteen

"Yeah! We don't know where's to go!" cried another.

The crowd grew restless. They shouted obscenities at Bait, criticizing everything about him, most painfully, his leadership skills. Reggie loved every second of it.

"All right! All right!" Bait whined, waving his arms up and down. "You don't like me, I get it! Now, shut up, or you's gonna get us all caught," he went on, keeping one eye on the theater. "What good is we if dem Sticks hears us?"

By some miracle, Bait's last comment managed to settle everyone down. They stopped berating him and agreed to listen. Even Reggie sat complacently, awaiting instructions. Raven, who was still puffing her fur back into shape, also seemed to be focusing.

"Okay, everyone, let's just get over der quickly," Bait continued. He made sure to speak fast before everyone started up again. "Just find yourselves anywhere dat Sticks can get out and stand der. If someone tries to leave, don't let 'em!"

"And how do we do dat?" Delio asked. "I mean, I know we's Alleys and stuff, but can't dey just leave from another spot? I mean, look at dat theater! Der's holes all over it! Da place looks like it's ready to fall down any second."

"Just do it, okay?" Bait sneered. "Why you's acting like such losers? You's Alleys, figure it out!"

"So, dat's it?" Tuesday asked. "We just stand in da same spot...all day?"

Life Eight

"Yeah, now where was you when I explained dis whole plan last night, huh?" Bait cracked. "Wasn't you listening to a word I said?"

"Of course I was, I just...well," Tuesday went on, "when do we get to go home? When do we get to eat, cause to tell you da truth, I could use a little breakfast."

"Breakfast? Breakfast?" cried Bait. "No one said nothin' about no breakfast!" Fact was, Bait's tummy was growling louder than anyone's. He could use a little mouse blood.

"Yeah, can't we get somethin' to eat first?" Steak called from the back of the group. "Ain't breakfast like da most important meal of da day?" he teased.

Once again, everyone shouted at Bait, growing more and more aggressive. It was ugly. There's nothing pretty about a tired, hungry group of Alleys. Standing upright with his arms over his chest, Reggie watched the show with selfish amusement. He just loved watching Bait squirm.

"Okay! Okay! We'll eat first!" Bait reluctantly agreed. It was never too hard to sway Bait in a different direction. "But don't tell Fidel! He'd want us at dat theater now! You hear me?"

Oh, we hear you, Bait," snapped Reggie. "Since you's so tired, why don't you stay here and rest? We'll bring you back something."

"Well, promise?" Bait wasn't sure if he could trust Reggie. His gut told him no, but the prospect of crawling back into that alley was too tempting to pass up.

"Promise," Reggie declared with the slightest glimmer of mischief in his eyes. "Would I ever lie to you, Bait? After all, you is kinda my boss, right?"

"I suppose," Bait said. He didn't know if it was his lack of sleep, food, or both that was clouding his judgment, but that tiny pea-brain of his sensed something wasn't right. "Just don't be too long, got it?"

"Of course, Bait," Reggie went on. "We've got too much work to do. We'll be back in a jiffy. You just rest, and I'll take care of everything."

"Okay, if you insists." Bait stretched out his lanky body. It crackled and creaked as he did. Without a second thought, he curled himself right back up into that same little ball he was in earlier. Within seconds, he was fast asleep. It was precious. Well, not really. This was Bait, after all.

"Come on, fellas!" Reggie cried. "Let's go get us some grub."

"Yeah!" everyone cheered.

Suddenly Raven stepped forward. "For da last time, I ain't no fella!"

"And you certainly ain't no lady either!" Reggie growled back at her.

"Well, I never!"

Reggie rolled his eyes. "Now why don't you go over der where you belong," he half ordered as he pointed at the rest of the Silent Five. "Haven't you noticed they's always very quiet and compliant?"

"What do you think I am, a dictionary?" Raven bolstered. "I don't know what all your fancy words mean!" She put her manicured paws to her hips and stuck out her bottom jaw like a snippy teenage girl would do.

"Awe, shut up and stand with da others before I gets really mad!" Reggie was starting to lose his cool, and the Silent Five were to never, never lose their cool. A sense of *cool* is what they supposedly were all about.

Reggie quickly pulled himself together. Taking in a long, deep breath, he puffed out his chest and shut his eyes. He knew he had to keep focused. There was a reason the Silent Five were labeled *silent*. Stay calm, stay quiet, and only act when told. That was their job.

"So are we getting' dat breakfast or what?" Tuesday called out over the hum of everyone's grumbling tummies. "We's starving over here!"

Reggie nodded his head and led the gang down the street. In a matter of minutes, they came to a promising alleyway. It was situated behind a small deli.

Delis always had lots of leftovers, even this early in the day. Sure enough, a concoction of delicious delicacies awaited. Sausage crumbles, leftover lox, and chunky chopped liver to name a few. In no time, they had the place cleaned out. Half eaten bagels, cheeses, leftover bacon and eggs... long gone. The food never stood a chance.

Feeling full and charged, Reggie led the Alleys back on the street, only he didn't take them back to Bait. It seemed he'd hatched himself another sort of plan.

Chapter Fourteen

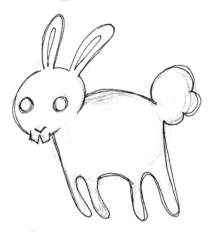

Later that day, Grim awoke from the most magnificent dream. A sense of calmness and clarity enveloped him. He was barely awake when he realized that his good mood hadn't been from a dream at all. It was real.

Lying in the crook of Dennis's elbow, Grim breathed in the delicious aroma that came with having Dennis beside him. Grim tilted his head just a smidge and looked right at Dennis's face. Seeing him so close, being so real, was a moment he would never forget.

Dennis was still asleep; his bandages wrapped around his head. His mouth was open just enough to detect a slight wheeze. With each exhale, Grim could feel his warm breath stroke the side of his face, gently blowing a few strands of his fur.

Life Eight

Grim gazed at Dennis like a little puppy dog. He could have stared at him all day. Time seemed to stop.

A little while later, it appeared Dennis was waking up. His feet started to wiggle, his arms stretched up, and he yawned wide. For fear of getting caught, Grim stuffed himself under the sheets, nestling himself in the bend of Dennis's knee. He lay there, shivering, trying desperately to think up a plan.

Before Grim had a chance to react, he could hear someone enter the room. Whoever it was, was dragging in some sort of cart. Grim could hear the wheels as they rotated across the floor.

"Yep, he's up," a woman's voice said. "The other one too. Both of them are up."

"Good, let's give 'em their meds," said another voice. "Their lunch'll be here soon, so let's get started."

Grim had forgotten there was another boy in the room. He had been so consumed with Dennis that he nearly forgot where he was. Taking a moment to get his mind clear, he wiggled away from Dennis's leg and thought hard. He seriously needed to figure out what he was going to do. After all, he couldn't just live under those covers forever. If one of the nurses found him, he'd be at the Pound in a flash. Keeping as still as he could, he waited for the right moment to leave.

"Here you go, Vinny," Grim heard the nurse say. Vinny was obviously the boy in the other bed.

"Your turn, Dennis," the second nurse said. "Pull up that sleeve."

"Okay, Bea," Dennis charmed. Grim hadn't heard Dennis's voice in forever. His heart sank at the sound of it. Even though his voice had deepened over the last few years, it was still Dennis. Grim would know that voice anywhere.

As Bea, the nurse, gave Dennis a hearty dose of pain meds in the fleshy part of his upper arm, his body stiffened. "Now, I need you boys to eat all your lunch today," Bea ordered. "You need to keep up your strength. These doctors'll never let you outta here without some strength in your bones."

The two nurses stood together at the end of Dennis's bed. Grim heard their footstep as they shuffled around in those big, white nurse's shoes. "These boys'll be seeing stars in a matter of minutes," Nurse Bea whispered to the other lady. "They won't know if they're coming or going."

"Should be a pretty good show," giggled the other nurse. "Maybe I'll check back in a few, you know, for a good laugh."

Grim didn't get it, but it wouldn't take long for him to figure out exactly what they meant by 'show'.

"Check out the bunnies on the ceiling!" Dennis cried. "They're all so cute! How do they do that without falling? And why are they purple?"

"I don't see any bunnies, Den," Vinny

said. "In fact, I don't even see a ceiling. Are you sure there is one?"

Now Grim understood. It was that pain medicine. It made them all loopy, like when someone's on the nip. Despite all Grim's downfalls, he had always stayed smart about that stuff. He'd never get himself on the nip. Many did. He had seen enough of them fall to ever get messed up in that junk.

"Oh, wow!" Dennis went on. "One of the bunnies is talking to me! But I can't speak Japanese! I wonder what he's saying!"

"You're messed up, Crumb," Vinny chuckled. "There ain't no bunnies. You're just hallucinating." He tilted his bandaged head up toward the ceiling. "The fact that you can't see all those hot air balloons up there proves it. I just wish you could see all those goats flying those balloons. It's pretty awesome!"

Grim could barely contain himself. He gnawed on his lip as much as he could to keep from laughing. These boys were gone, far gone. So gone, in fact, he wondered when and if they'd ever come back.

Keeping his place under the sheets, Grim waited for the boys to quiet down, but there was one problem, he was getting very hot. He could barely breathe, let alone keep quiet. All the huffing and puffing he was about to do would get him noticed for sure. He had just decided make his escape, when something Dennis said caught his attention.

Chapter Fourteen

"Boy, Vin, I'm starting to think this medicine is making me feel funny," Dennis began. "My teeth are fuzzy, my toes itch, and it's like everything is blurry. I don't even know what I'm looking at. There could be a vampire in here for all I know."

"Weird, I know," Vinny agreed. "I'm just trying to figure out what all those balloons are doing up there."

Taking a big chance, Grim decided to do the unthinkable. Slowly and carefully, he crawled his way up Dennis's body and poked his head out of the sheet. In one swift move, he curled himself alongside Dennis and lay his head down on his chest. Letting out a slow, deep breath, he waited. His heart was racing.

Feeling the soft, warm fur on his body, Dennis quickly turned his head. The surprised look on his face sent Grim's mind spinning. Maybe this was a very bad mistake.

"Romeo, is that you?" Dennis suddenly cried. "It's really you! It's really you!"

Grim's heart stopped. His body started to sweat. Was this happening? Was Dennis really talking to him?

"Oh, Romeo, Romeo, I've missed you so!" Dennis cried as he scooped him up into his arms. "I can't believe this! I just can't believe it! It's really you, isn't it?" He blinked his bloodshot eyes about a thousand times just to make sure. He twisted Grim around and sure enough, found his signature diamond mark. "Yes, it is you! It

Life Eight

is you!" Dennis brought Grim closer to his face and smothered him in kisses. "Don't ever leave me again! My little Romeo's back! He's back! Oh my God!"

Grim purred his heart out. He had dreamed of this moment a million times. It was a dream come true. He could barely contain himself.

"Romeo, I love you!" Dennis cried, holding Grim tightly against his chest. "I love you so much! I'm so sorry for everything I've done! I'm so sorry! I'm so sorry!"

"Who in the world are you talking to?" rang Vinny's voice over the curtain. "You sound like you're in a soap opera! Are you cracking up or something?"

"Naw, this is just my best friend, Romeo," Dennis cried, tears streaming down his face. "He's back! He's back! I didn't kill him! Come take a look for yourself! He's real! He's really real!"

"Romeo? You mean your dead cat?" Vinny pestered. "You're losing it for sure, Crumb. You can keep talking to your zombie cat, but I'm gonna get a little shut eye, if you don't mind. Besides, I can't really move. I'm like a mummy over here, if you haven't noticed."

"Sure, whatever," Dennis grumbled, still holding onto his cat for dear life. He looked into Grim's big eyes and said again, "Romeo, I love you."

Grim continued to purr loud and strong, letting Dennis know just how happy he was.

Life Eight

It was all he could do to keep from losing it completely.

Dennis was awfully calm, perhaps a little too calm, but Grim didn't care. He was lying with him just like he used to. It was so nice. The love he felt for this boy was a love like no other. He had never before and would never again feel for anyone the way he felt for Dennis. As much as he loved Queen Elizabeth, his father, and all his former friends, the connection between a pet and its owner is priceless. Even he couldn't understand it sometimes.

Sadly, Grim knew all too well this moment wouldn't last. It couldn't. Sooner or later, Dennis would snap out of his medically induced fog, and Grim would have to go. There was just no other way. But for the time being, Grim took in every moment like it was their last. For all he knew, it was.

Chapter Fifteen

The gang at the Hope Street Theater was well into another busy day. Candle and some of the other females resumed their work organizing and decorating the old dressing rooms. Mr. Shadow was busily jotting down ideas for the new and improved Stick School. Even Roy and Yellowtail were hard at work. They had a particularly good morning at the docks, providing everyone with a healthy and hearty lunch. Big delicious meals like this were few and far between these days, but on those off chances when things went their way, everyone walked around a little happier. Even Fluffy.

"Hi, Mr. Shadow!" Fluffy called, simply bursting with positive energy. "What you got planned for the day? Painting? Decorating? Lesson planning?"

"Boy, son, you sure are in a good mood,"

Shadow said. "Just what are you up to, huh? *Huh?*"

"Oh, calm it, Mr. Shadow," Fluffy teased. "I know I've been a bit of a nuisance lately, but that's all in the past. I'm a new male today. I feel it!"

Shadow stepped a little closer to Fluffy, trying to get a good long look into his eyes. If he didn't see some clarity, then perhaps Fluffy's sudden switch-a-roo was not very organic.

"What do you mean, you're a new male?" Shadow asked, searching Fluffy's eyes for signs of nip. "What happened to you? Are you all right? Do you need a doctor?"

"Hardly! I'm just feeling great, that's all!"

"Seriously now, son," Shadow pestered on. "What's gotten into you? Just the other day you were arguing with Mr. Sox like you were top Stick. Now I'm only going to ask you one more time, what's going on?"

"Oh, okay, old fella," Fluffy teased. "If you insist."

"I do."

"Well, it's just like you said," Fluffy explained. "Fighting with Sox. What was I thinking?" He paused a moment and sat down. With his tail wrapped around his body, he said, "I was thinking a lot about what Sox said to me, you know, about Fidel."

"What did he say again?" Shadow asked. "I, uh, guess I forgot."

"He said all that stuff about not living

in constant worry about Fidel," Fluffy repeated with passion. "I realized that I've been doing just that. Every move I make is somehow related to Fidel and his whereabouts. Well, I'm done with all that. I'm not going to worry about it another second! And you know what?"

"What?"

"I feel free. Yep, free!" Fluffy did a little dance around the lobby of the theater. "I just wish I had thought of this sooner."

"Well, I'm happy you've had this little ah-ha moment," Shadow said, "but it's time to get back to work! We've got a theater to clean! Now, go do something useful before I get really mad!"

Fluffy walked off with a huge grin on his face. He was feeling good, perhaps a little too good. It seemed he had Mr. Shadow convinced, but would the others buy his new attitude?

"Hey, Mr. Sox!" Fluffy called, seeing the old man standing alone on the stage. "This is some room, ain't it, Sox?"

"I beg your pardon, Mr. Fluffy?" Sox asked.

"This must've been a remarkable theater, don't you think?" Fluffy took a slow walk toward the stage. "I can just imagine this room when it was new. The paint, these murals, all this amazing architecture," he went on, marveling at the intricate etchings all along the wooden molding. "It's just so sad now. I can't believe the people let this happen to such a beautiful place."

"Things do happen, Fluffy," Mr. Sox

explained. "You know that truth better than most." Sox walked carefully to the edge of the large stage and sat down. He watched as Fluffy wove in and out of some of the aisles, taking his time as he fantasized about what must have been a grand place and time.

"Do you think it'll ever be like that again, Mr. Sox?" Fluffy asked, a dreamy look in his eyes.

"Like what, Fluffy? Like what?"

"You know, this place, the city," Fluffy said, his eyes darting around the massive room, "the whole world! Do you think it'll ever be good, like it used to be before any of us could even remember?"

Mr. Sox pushed his little glasses down a bit lower on his nose. Gently he brushed the grey fur on his head from his eyes. He cleared his old, rusty throat and said, "No, Fluffy. I don't."

"Really? You don't think this could all come back some day?"

"No, I really don't." Sox stood up, and also took a moment to glance around the room. A melancholy look swept across his face. "What's gone is gone. There's no bringing back the past. Oh, sure, there may be good times again in this city, and surely for us, but the golden age is gone. The people, they let it happen."

"But why? How?"

"It's about money. It's always been about money."

Chapter Fifteen

Fluffy hopped up onto the stage and sat beside his mentor. "Oh, that's really too bad. It's a shame these old places have to die like this."

"Yes, Fluffy, it is," Sox said. It was clear in his tone he wasn't entirely buying this whole conversation. He found Fluffy's mood strange and was waiting for the right moment to question him. After all, this was the very place Fluffy lost his most recent life. Surely Fluffy hadn't forgotten so quickly. "So, Fluffy," he asked, ready to make his move, "what's with all the questions? Are you feeling all right? You were so angry with me the other day, I just wanted to make sure we're okay."

"Oh, sure, everything's cool," Fluffy said with a questionable smile. "Like we talked about the other day, I get it. I get the whole Fidel thing."

"What Fidel thing?"

"You know, all that stuff about not living in fear of him. Not letting him control our lives. You remember saying all that, right?"

"Of course, of course I remember," Mr. Sox said emphatically. "I just hope you really mean it. That you truly agree with me."

Fluffy faced the house seats, stood on his hind legs, and put his arms up over his head in a large V shape and said convincingly, "I'm a new male, Mr. Sox, and it's all thanks to you. I don't care about Fidel, the rats, the Dogs, the Pound, ghosts, any of it! Nothing can touch me! Just you watch and see!"

Mr. Sox slowly approached Fluffy and put

 148

his paw to his shoulder. "That's great, Fluffy, really great. Just don't get yourself too carried away, okay?"

"Got it." Fluffy watched as Mr. Sox disappeared off the stage. Now standing alone in the large room, Fluffy took in a deep breath and sat back down. It was true, what he was saying. He had come to an epiphany since the last meeting, and ever since then had felt fearless. It was only as he glanced up and caught sight of the lighting booth that his confidence began to waver. Images of Ned the ghost flashed in his mind. He could envision himself crashing down on the stage again and again. Then he began to wonder, how does one protect himself from vengeful ghosts?

Chapter Sixteen

After a good, long nap, Grim awoke beside Dennis. Marvelous. In his sleep he had moved himself back under the hospital sheets. Dennis was still sleeping, and so was Vinny, his friend and roommate.

Once again, Grim could hear some voices in the room. He wasn't sure who they belonged to, so he stayed as still as he could. As always, he knew under no circumstances, could he get caught. His greatest worry. He prayed Dennis wasn't getting examined. That would give him away for sure.

"Doctor, when can Dennis come home?" asked a woman. She sounded nervous and distressed. "I want to bring him home."

I know that voice, Grim thought to himself. *That's Mrs. Crumb.*

Life Eight

"Mrs. Crumb, I promise Dennis will go home as soon as his body is healed enough," the doctor said. He had a low, monotone voice that sounded somewhat patronizing.

"But when will that be, Doctor? His father and I can't hardly stand it anymore!" Mrs. Crumb pleaded.

"Like I already told you, Mrs. Crumb, when he's ready." The doctor paused. Grim could hear what sounded like shuffling papers. "It says right here on the chart, Mrs. Crumb, that your son suffered a very serious head injury. Head injuries are tricky. They need time and care to heal properly. Even though he's doing well now, things could suddenly change. You don't want him going home too soon, do you?" he asked in that same condescending way. "You wouldn't want him suffering from some after effect because you want to take him home and make him chicken soup and dumplings."

"What? Of course not, Doctor," Mrs. Crumb said. Her voice started to shake, and it sounded like she was crying. "I just want to know he's going to get better, that's all. I worry about him. He's my only child."

"We're taking very good care of Dennis and his friends, Mrs. Crumb," the doctor said, his voice warming a bit.

"Thank you, Doctor," Mrs. Crumb said with a sniffle. "I know you're taking good care of my little boy."

"Yes, yes indeed I am," he went on. "Now,

why don't you run along home. I'll call you if I need to. Dennis is just going to sleep for a little while longer."

"I thought I'd just stay a bit and wait for Dennis to wake up, so I can…"

"There's really no need, Mrs. Crumb," the doctor remarked. "When he gets up, I've got some tests I want to do, so it's really best that you just head on home. Trust me, I promise to call you if anything should come up."

"Okay, Doctor, I guess you know what's best."

"Thank you, Mrs. Crumb. Bye, bye, now," the doctor said as he patted her shoulder.

Grim could hear the clunk of Mrs. Crumb's shoes walk out of the room. They sounded like old lady shoes.

Grim felt badly for Mrs. Crumb. Even though the doctor softened, he didn't like the way he talked to her, like she was a child. Where was his compassion? Where was his understanding? And by the way, what kind of tests was he planning on doing?

Grim stayed still under the sheets. Suddenly, he heard more footsteps enter the room. These shoes sounded different. Rubber soles.

"Is there anything I can get you, Doctor?" another familiar voice asked. "I'm going on my break soon, and I thought I'd check in before I left."

"Maybe just a stiff drink, Nurse Bea," the

doctor teased. Grim could hear the two of them laughing. "Seriously, these mothers are driving me off the wall. Why can't they just leave me alone to do my job? Why must they question me so?"

Grim couldn't believe what he was hearing? This was the doctor who was helping Dennis? Grim dug his claws into the plastic hospital mattress to keep from pouncing on the doctor's face.

"Oh, Doctor, you know they're just concerned about their children," the nurse said. "They don't mean any harm."

"I know." The doctor glanced over at his young, innocent patients. "Their pain meds will be wearing off. Let's wait until after lunch to do the tests. They'll be up and coherent by then."

"Got it, sir," Nurse Bea agreed. "After lunch. Speaking of which, wanna join me? I'm heading to the cafeteria now."

"Don't mind if I do," the doctor charmed. "Lead the way, Nurse Bea. I'm right behind you."

Grim heard all four shoes exit the room, then exhaled a big sigh of relief. He hadn't been caught, not yet at least. Just as he was relaxing a little, he remembered something the doctor had said. *"Their meds will be wearing off."* What could *that mean?* And then it dawned on him. Dennis would be waking up any minute. *He'll freak when he sees me! Without the meds making him loopy, he'll definitely freak!*

Chapter Sixteen

Grim knew he had to get out of there. Meds aside, he had to pee, and humans always picked up on the stinging smell of cat pee. But how would he escape? It was the middle of the day. The hospital was teaming with people. News crews, family, doctors and nurses. A far cry from the quiet somber of the nighttime skeleton crew. Getting out would be tricky, but he knew he could do it.

I'll come back tonight, Grim told himself. *When less people are around and when Dennis is back on his meds for the night.* It warmed his body just to imagine lying beside Dennis for another night. It was truly a dream come true.

Knowing the doctor would be returning soon, Grim searched for his escape. With his head peeking out from the sheet, he watched the door for any unexpected visitors. He could see partially down the hall. It was all clear.

Grim wiggled his way out of the sheets and sat up tall. Dennis was asleep beside him. His little snore reminded Grim of the many nights he took for granted growing up in the Crumb home. So many days and nights with Dennis. Will he ever have that again?

The hallway was the only way out. Going out the window, Grim's *go-to* escape plan, would be impossible. There were no trees to help him down. It was a straight fall, and considering everything he had ever been through, jumping just was not an option.

Grim slowly pulled himself to a standing

154

position. Keeping his eyes on Dennis, he tiptoed to the edge of the bed. With his paws up on the protective rails, he was about to leap off when Dennis started to wake up. Dennis rustled around for a moment, smacked his mouth open and closed, and started to groan. Grim knew nothing about head injuries, but if he were to guess, seeing your dead pet in your hospital bed just might lead to more trauma. He could only let Dennis see him when he was under the medicine, when his mind wasn't all there.

Thinking fast, Grim dashed under the bed. Good thing he did, for in just another moment, Dennis was fully awake. Grim positioned himself behind some sort of medical equipment to keep himself hidden. Unfortunately for him, the floor was sticky and covered in some sort of slime. It would be a miracle if he came out of there without an unknown ailment. Practically stuck to the tiles, he listened as Dennis started talking.

You awake, Vin?" Dennis asked. His voice sounded warm and healthy. Maybe he would be going home soon. "Vinny, are you up?"

"What's the big idea, Crumb?" cried a very groggy and annoyed Vinny. "I was asleep."

"Sorry buddy, but I had the weirdest dream."

"Yeah, well, you gonna tell me what it was, or just keep me in suspense?" jabbed Vinny.

Vinny couldn't see Dennis rolling his eyes at him. They were separated by a curtain, after all. "I dreamed my old cat, Romeo, was here," he said softly. "Right here in the bed with me, but it was only a dream. He's dead, you know. Weird, huh?"

"What's weird is a grown boy who still dreams about his little kitty cat," Vinny meowed over and over.

"Awe, don't be like that," Dennis said. "Seriously, it was so real, it didn't seem like a dream at all. It was like he was really here." Grim could feel his heart warm deep in his chest. It was a good feeling.

"So you had a dream about your dead kitty," Vinny grumbled. "Big deal. When you have a dream about Veronica Whippleworth, maybe I'll listen."

"Veronica from school? The cheerleader?"

"Yeah, that's the one," Vinny said, sounding a little more alert.

"Oh, well, she's in my math class and…"
And just like that, the conversation about him was over. Just the mention of a pretty girl, and he was out of Dennis's mind once again. With his head low, Grim crawled out from under the bed and rushed to the door.

Luckily, the hallway was still clear. Grim knew he had to get out the same way he got in. Taking in a deep breath, he ran as fast as he could. After a few near misses, ducking into supply closets and hiding in laundry carts, he was safely back outside. Thank goodness visiting hours hadn't started yet. For now, the halls were devoid of people.

Standing there in the cold, only one thought came to Grim's mind. *Now what?*

 156

Chapter Seventeen

The Hope Street Theater was hopping. Lots of Sticks had gathered, more than usual. It was Tabitha's birthday, and everyone wanted to celebrate.

While the Sticks went blindly along with their business of preparing for the birthday party and cleaning the theater, they had no idea their precious new haven was completely surrounded by Alleys. There was no way in, no way out. Of all the Alleys present, Bait was not one of them. Still asleep in the alleyway across the street, he would have a rude awakening, that is, when he actually woke up.

"So what else do we need to do for the party?" Darla asked Candle in the privacy of her own room, a former dressing room. "Is there food? Favors? A cake?"

Chapter Fifteen

"You are very sweet to think of all those things," Candle said warmly, "but as you know, we don't have much. I did think we could all gather on the stage and sing a happy birthday song. Unfortunately, that will have to do as her gift."

The Sticks were never much into birthdays anyway. Because of all their different lives, it often just got too confusing. A simple gathering and perhaps a small gift was about it.

"That's okay," Darla said. "We don't need to do much. The song should be just fine. We are together, after all."

"Well, almost all of us are here," Candle frowned.

"Who's not here?" Darla asked. She paused, noticed Candle's sad eyes, then said, "Oh, you do know that Fluffy *is* here, right?"

Candle looked up at Darla with puffy, red eyes. "Oh, Fluffy, yes, I know he's here. That's good."

"Then why are you sad, Candle? Who else could you be talking about?"

Darla's lack of insight surprised Candle. Still, Darla didn't feel the same way as she did. "Romeo's not here," Candle whispered. "I wish he was."

"Romeo? Well, you remember he's gone, right?" Darla reminded. All the Sticks believed that Romeo had died all his remaining lives at the Asian restaurant from being thrown into the hot, boiling oil. That was the last they knew of him. Of course, it was surviving that incident that gave life to Romeo's alter ego Grim, the deformed alley cat turned Troop member.

"I know he's gone, Darla," Candle said softly. "I guess I still think of him though. I miss him, that's all."

"Well, even if he was here, you do remember how impossible he had gotten?" Darla added. "I mean, I don't know that I would want him here, even if he was alive."

"I know, I know, but all that stuff," Candle went on, "I just wish I had another chance to help him through it. He was a good guy. He really was."

While Darla and Candle continued their conversation, Mr. Sox was busy overseeing the stage clean up in preparation for Tabitha's celebration. As he watched Snickers and Uncle Fred attempt to sweep the dusty, wooden floor, he too thought about someone who would not be in attendance…Romeo.

Mr. Sox was the only Stick who knew that Romeo was still alive. The whole time Sox was locked in the Fourth Corner dungeon, he knew that Grim, newest member of the Silent Five, was really his once trusted friend. Sox didn't understand how Romeo ended up working at the dungeon or why. He also didn't understand that Romeo was secretly trying to help him all that time, or maybe he did. Either way, keeping this information to himself was difficult, but he knew there was no reason to share it at this time. The news would only shock and possibly traumatize his family of Sticks. For now, he had no intention of telling anyone. Even he wanted to forget.

"I think we're ready, Mr. Sox," Candle said as she came bouncing onto the stage. She had the ability to go into denial about anything bothering her and resume a more pleasant attitude. It truly was a gift. "Should I get Tabitha?"

Mr. Sox stood motionless at the center of the stage. It worried Candle.

"Mr. Sox, are you all right?" she questioned as she moved closer to him. "I said, are you all right?"

"Yes, yes, my dear," Sox finally said, still deep in thought over the one Stick he somehow failed. "Go get Tabitha. That will be fine."

Candle took a step back. She knew when Mr. Sox wanted to be alone. "Okay, I'll just go get her. I guess we'll all be here soon for the party. Okay?"

"Yes, yes, child. Go ahead."

As Candle walked away, Mr. Sox let his head drop a little lower. Thinking of Romeo, he had worked himself into quite a depression. *Where did I go wrong, Romeo?* he wondered. *Where did I go wrong?*

Outside the theater, Reggie and the others secured any possible entrance they could. Being given no solid instructions on where to stand, they took it upon themselves to find their stations. Of course, Reggie oversaw the entire

Life Eight

operation, never once thinking of Bait.

Bait slept soundly on his little garbage can lid in the alley across the street. Still snoring away, he had no idea the very Alleys he was in charge of had already begun the mission Fidel had entrusted to him. There was no telling what Bait would do to Reggie once he finally awoke. Luckily for Reggie, the possibility of that was growing narrower and narrower. A pack of Dogs had just entered the alley, and they looked angry.

"Whatawe have here?" cried one of the Dogs. "A sweet, little pussy cat!"

"Awe, ain't that somethin'," cracked another. "It's an awful shame we're gonna have to mess him up!"

Bait opened his eyes, which was hard to do with all the crust that had formed on his lids during his nap. With his paw, he wiped it all away and let his eyes begin to focus. As his vision cleared, he was horrified to see three big Dogs surrounding him in a semi-circle. They were tall and husky. Their large, red eyes burned right through him. His face glistened in their sharp teeth. Bait quickly looked around for Reggie and the other Alleys, but they were nowhere to be found.

"Now come on fellas," slurred Bait. "I don't want no trouble!"

One of the Dogs smiled a very menacing smile as he leaned closer to Bait's face. "You don't want any trouble, do you?" the mutt snickered. "We don't plan on being any trouble, now do we boys?"

"Naw, not at all," the others teased, also with the same devious grin.

Bait began to scramble out of the metal lid. Still on his bottom, he crawled backwards keeping his eyes on the Dogs. "I'm just gonna go about my business, okay fellas? You go right back to whatever you was doin', and I'll be outta here in a jiffy. Got it?"

"Oh, we *got it,* all right," the first Dog teased. "You're trespassing!"

"Trespassing? I ain't trespassing!" roared Bait, still inching away. "Dis here is an alley, and I'm an Alley, so you is the ones trespassing!"

"Oh, is dat so?"

"Yeah, it's so! No Dogs allowed in da alleys, right?" Bait snarled.

"Says who?"

"Says me!" Although Bait was holding it together, he was trembling inside something awful. Being alone in an alley with three big Dogs was not a good situation, unless you're a Dog.

"Hey, Mutt!" yelled one of the Dogs. "Dis guy says no Dogs allowed in alleys! Whataya think of dat?"

"I tink we gotta teach dis guy a lesson," answered the other Dog.

"Yeah, a lesson!"

Bait gulped. This wasn't going to be good. He scrambled for an idea. Maybe he could convince them he was a Stick. The Dogs and

Life Eight

the Sticks had been friendly ever since Pierre the poodle and his pals helped the Sticks chase the Alleys out of the Factory a few years back. Unfortunately for Bait, the Dogs still blame the Alleys for killing one of their own. For that reason, the Dogs remained enemies with the Alleys. They were and always would be enemies. Besides, Bait already told them himself that he was an Alley.

"Now, come on you guys," Bait said slowly, quickly realizing the seriousness of the situation. He knew this couldn't possibly end well. To top it off, he had no idea if he was a niner or not. The number nine was much too big for him to keep track of. "Why don't we just say our goodbyes and forget I was ever here, okay? Would dat work for you?"

But the Dogs kept coming…closer and closer. Their growls grew lower and faster. Drool pelted from their mouths like hail. Their eyes burned with rage.

Bait moved farther and farther away from the street and deeper and deeper into the alley as he tried to keep his distance from the Dogs. But it wasn't working. He had to move in the other direction if he had any chance at all. As dumb as he was, he was smart enough to know that he was no match for these canine creatures. They were bigger and stronger than him, and it was three against one. Keeping his wits about him, which was not an easy thing for Bait to do, he scanned the alley for an escape. And then, just as he was almost to the back wall, he spotted something that gave him an idea.

Stacked all the way up the wall was a bunch of old boxes. At the top of these boxes was a ladder bolted into the bricks that allowed the service workers to come and go. These ladders went all the way up the 5-story building.

The Dogs were nearly nose-to-nose with Bait, when he decided to make a run for it. "Well, it's been nice chattin' with you fellas, but I gots to go!" As fast as he could, Bait zipped his way up the boxes, digging his claws into the soggy cardboard and hanging on just long enough to reach the next. Down below, the Dogs howled up at him with evil, threatening cries.

"Get back here!" howled one of the Dogs. "We ain't finished with you!"

Standing at the top box, Bait looked down at the three mangy mutts glaring up at him. "Ha! Ha! You fellas are messin' with da wrong cat!" he roared. "I bet you feel pretty darn stupid right about now."

Down on the ground the Dogs paced angrily. "Who you callin' stupid?" one of them shouted.

Balancing on the top box, Bait did a little victory dance, taunting the Dogs with his evil laughter. "Na-na-na-na-na! I fooled you!"

As Bait grinned from ear to ear, the Dogs came up with an idea of their own. "Hey kitty!" they all yelled up at him.

"Kitty? That's a laugh!" Bait chuckled.

"Laugh, eh? How'd you like some of dis?"

Life Eight

the biggest Dog cried as he swung at the first row of boxes, knocking them out of the way.

"Uh-oh," Bait sighed. Seeing his doom hanging before him, he quickly reached for the ladder. Mere inches away, he almost had it. Just a little bit farther! As he stretched his skinny arm as far as it would go, the boxes fell from under him. Before he had time to think, he was plummeting down to the ground.

Screaming like a little girl, Bait fell fast. Below him, the three Dogs cheered and hollered. Through his fear, Bait could see them clearly as they grew bigger and bigger. Their eyes lit up, and they rubbed their front paws together in anticipation.

With a thud only a cat could survive, Bait landed. Bouncing up on all fours, he didn't waste a moment. Like lightning, he bolted through the Dogs and rushed toward the street, making it out by the skin of his nose. The Dogs were left to wallow in a thick cloud of dust. They knew they'd get to him later. There was always later.

Bait ran across the street. The Hope Street Theater was right in front of him. Pausing to catch his breath, he looked back at the alleyway. To both his delight and surprise, he saw all three Dogs walking the other way.

Dat's what I thought," Bait whispered to himself, feeling like a big shot. "You fellas just get outta here. Nobody wants no Dogs around."

Bait took a moment to study the theater. Standing on the sidewalk by the front entrance,

Chapter Seventeen

he peered up at the old wonder. The faded Hope Street Theater sign hung to its last rusty nail as if it were hanging on for dear life. "What a dump," Bait whispered. "Who'd wanna live here anyway?" Of course, Bait would never admit it, but he was probably a little jealous of the Sticks. After all, he had lived in some of the dirtiest, nastiest alleyways in the city.

I better go check out where the rest of dose lowlifes is, Bait thought. *Dey better not be up to anything stupid.* Bait was oblivious to the fact that they had all left him asleep in the alley. They didn't bring him any food as they had said they would, and they certainly hadn't waited for him. At some point their disloyalty would sink in, but for now, he hadn't a clue.

Bait wandered around the exterior of the theater. It was not a freestanding building but was attached on one side to an office building. On the other side of the theater was an alley. This was not the typical creepy, dark alley. It was a pleasant, open area where theatergoers used to hang out and smoke during intermission, but had become like the rest of the property, rundown and neglected. Behind the theater was another alley, the very alley where Candle and Fluffy had their date.

Bait wandered around the side of the theater where the smokers hung out. No one was there. He was about to turn around and head the other way, when he heard voices. Curious as always, he followed them. Soon, he came upon Reggie talking to some other Alleys. He crouched down low and listened.

"So, you guys just stay here, okay?" Reggie said. "If any Sticks try to get through even this little spot here," he explained, pointing to a small crack between some bricks, "you stop 'em. No Sticks in. No Sticks out. Dat's what Fidel wants."

"Is we gonna do like a big explosion or something?" asked Steak, who was part of the team involved in the giant cat tree fiasco. They pretended the tree was a gift, a peace offering to the Sticks. Once they successfully tricked Uncle Fred into bringing it inside the Factory, they burst out of the makeshift tree like a Trojan horse and ransacked the place. "Is der gonna be something like dat?"

"Naw, we ain't pulling any stunts dis time," Reggie explained. "We just gonna hang here until Fidel gives us our orders. We'll work in shifts though, you know, so you can poop and stuff."

"All right, so I guess if I sees someone, I'll clobber 'em, is dat it?" Steak asked, feeling a little unclear about what he was supposed to do.

"Sure, yeah, take 'em down," Reggie agreed.

Hiding a few feet away, Bait couldn't believe what he was hearing. "Come on, Reggie, you can do better than dat!" he cried as he came bounding in.

"I beg your pardon?" Reggie replied. He

had been expecting Bait. There was only so long he could sleep in that alley.

"It don't sound like you gots much of a plan there, do ya?" Bait teased.

"Oh, yeah?" Reggie snorted. "You got somethin' better to say?"

Bait cleared his throat and took a step closer. He kicked his brain into high gear and basically repeated Reggie's exact instructions. "Just take 'em down if you see any. Now *dat's* how you explain a plan," he snapped with a glare to Reggie.

Reggie waited for Bait to walk away. Once he finally did, he took a moment to shake his head. "He's nuts," he said to the others. "I don't know how he got his job in da first place."

Reggie walked around the theater checking all the possible hiding spots. He planted several of the recruited Alleys in and around these locations and confirmed his instructions to bring down any Stick trying to get in or out of the building. All there was to do now was wait. And that's exactly what he did.

Chapter Eighteen

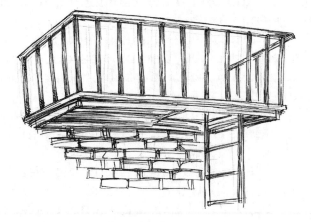

Grim wandered the streets for a little while before deciding to head back to the hoarder's house. He knew Terrence and Miles were probably worried about him. He also knew he no longer looked like Grim. That in itself was dangerous. The Alleys would tear him apart, and the Sticks would be furious, or so he imagined. He also needed to return to his new title as Troop member. Surely they would be expecting him. He was, after all, sort of their leader.

"Hey, Grim!" Miles called as he saw him enter the messy backyard. "Where you been? Did you see your boy?"

A smile ran across Grim's face. "Yes, I saw him," he said. In his mind he was still lying beside Dennis with his head on his lap. It

Chapter Eighteen

had been a dream come true. "I spent the night in the hospital, in his bed and everything."

"How's dat possible?" Miles asked. He knew all too well how dangerous that could have been. "You didn't get caught, did you?"

"Naw, I was careful enough," Grim affirmed. "Besides, Dennis was doped up on so much medicine, he probably thought he was dreaming."

"Yeah, he probably won't remember a thing," Miles chuckled. "He probably forgot all about you by now."

"Maybe," Grim sighed, his head low from just the thought of it. "I guess, maybe."

"So, how's he doing? Is he all right and stuff?" Miles asked as delicately as he could.

Grim paused a moment. Imagining Dennis in that hospital bed with all that equipment and all those bandages was not an easy task. "He's okay. I heard the doctor say that his head injuries are bad, but he should be going home soon."

"Are you going back there?"

"Tonight. I'm going back tonight. I'm going to stay the night again."

"Do you think dat's such a good idea?" Miles asked, thinking only of Grim's safety.

Grim looked him straight in the eye. "It's the best idea I've ever had."

"Okay, then."

Grim walked away from Miles and found himself a few soggy scraps of something to eat.

Life Eight

As always, Maxi, the hoarder, hadn't left out much cat food. Fending for themselves had become the norm for the Troops.

Grim saw several of them mulling around, hanging out, chasing bugs, that sort of thing. For whatever reason, he had no interest in meeting any of them. The only cat he had any real interest in other than Terrence and Miles was Roger, the supposed long, lost son of Fidel. Anxious to learn more about his story, Grim set out to find him.

After wandering around the yard, Grim made the difficult decision to search inside the house. That's where Roger usually was. Like Maxi, he too was a hoarder. He liked living in her junk, literally. It gave him a sense of comfort and belonging. While he didn't actually hoard much himself, her hoard fulfilled the piece of him that was broken.

Inside the house, Grim walked carefully from room to room searching for Roger. Getting around was always a challenge. There was hardly any floor space, let alone any space at all.

Grim climbed his way over the boxes and garbage, the piles of furniture and stacks of books. He kept a sharp eye out for Maxi. After all, she did bury him. *I looked like Grim then*, he remembered. He looked like Romeo now. Even if Maxi did see him, she wouldn't recognize him. Still, she was so unstable, he knew it was best to stay away.

Chapter Eighteen

After about half an hour, Grim decided Roger wasn't home. Making his way back outside, he quickly found Miles. "Hey, Miles, seen Roger?"

"Roger? Oh, I believe he went to look for you," Miles remember. "He was with Terrence, I think."

"Do you remember where they were going? I have something I want to ask him."

Miles could sense something was up, but he wasn't sure what. "Is it something I could help you with?" he asked.

"No, it has to do with Fidel, his father," Grim replied. He looked up into the cloudy sky as his mind wandered off in another direction. Fidel. All these years and it was still all about Fidel.

"Oh, okay."

"Do you remember anything?" Grim was getting agitated. And he was very obvious about it. He began to pace back and forth in front of Miles and breathe heavily.

Miles closed his eyes to think. "I do remember hearing them say something about a theater. Could dat be your theater? Da one for da Sticks?"

"Yes! That must be the Hope Street Theater!" Grim cried. "Now, why would they be looking for me there?" He squinted his eyes and continued to pace. "Maybe they thought I was going to check in on the Sticks? Or maybe they thought since I don't look like

 172

Life Eight

Grim anymore, I was going to tell the Sticks all about where I've been?"

"I got no idea," Miles said with a shrug of his shoulders. "Why don't you go and check it out for yourself?"

"I think I will." Grim stepped away.

"Hey, can I go with you?" Miles asked. "I'll help you look for dem."

Grim paused. He usually preferred to do this sort of thing on his own, but being a good friend, Grim decided to let Miles come along. "Sure, just follow me. Do you remember where it is?"

"Of course I do," Miles chuckled. "I'm an Alley. I know where everything is."

Grim and Miles started toward the theater. As they walked, Grim thought about what he would do once he got there. His gut instinct told him not to go anywhere near that theater. He didn't want to be discovered by any of the Sticks, not yet, at least.

Deep in the crevices of his mind, Grim figured someday, somehow, he'd sit with them all again. He'd explain his experience in Grimsville, the hot oil that disfigured him, leaving him no choice but to change his name to Grim. Using his misfortune to his advantage, he entered the Fourth Corner cave during a terrible rainstorm. He'd tell them about the death of his father, the release of Mr. Sox from the Fourth Corner dungeon, and his brief career as a member of Fidel's

173

Chapter Eighteen

Silent Five. Of course, he'd discuss his role in Fidel's escape from the theater and his life as a Troop member. For Grim, all that seemed so long ago, another lifetime perhaps. For now, the question remained...would any of them understand?

"Let's just go check this out real quick," Grim shouted back to Miles who was two steps behind him. "If we don't see them right away, we're leaving. I want to get back to the hospital before visiting hours."

"Sure, Grim," Miles agreed. "Let's make dis quick. We don't wanna get you caught."

"Right."

The two friends stayed quiet during their walk. Both deep in thought, they pressed their noses to the ground, moving quickly and cautiously. The ice was nearly melted, but the streets and sidewalks were slushy and slippery. Plus, Grim had to be extra alert for anyone who might recognize him.

As they approached the Hope Street Theater, Grim and Miles discussed their last minute plan. "Let's not get too close," Grim suggested. "I just want to get a quick look, see what's been going on since the last time I was here when we all had the fight." He paused a moment to remember that dreadful day. His fight with Fluffy still haunted him, as did the memory of Ned, the ghost. "If Terrence or Roger are here, hopefully they'll be in a spot where we can see them."

Life Eight

"Yes, I hope so," Miles said. He looked over at Grim, whom he admired so, and asked, "Are you gonna tell me about Dennis? Is he gonna get better or what?"

"Dennis seems all right, I guess," Grim said softly. "I want to get back there right away. I had a funny feeling after I left. I don't know why, I just did."

"Well, let's find those two and get outta here," Miles added. "I don't want any trouble. I'm too tired for trouble."

"I agree with that," Grim teased.

Grim and Miles were now very close to the theater. As they walked up the street, they could see its ornate rooftop creeping above the buildings. "It is beautiful, isn't it?" Miles said. "Reminds me of the kinda place Fifi and I were gonna settle in. Something just like that."

Not sure what to say, Grim gave Miles a small smile. He really didn't know what else to do.

Grim quickly searched for a hiding spot where he would both be safe and have a good, clear view of the theater. After a quick look around, he found the perfect place. "There! Let's get up there!" he cried, pointing at a small, four-story apartment building just kiddy-corner to the theater. "We'll climb to the top, then we'll be able to see the whole theater."

"Climb to the top?" Miles asked with a

shudder in his voice. He wasn't in the mood for a climb. "You sure about that?"

"Sure I'm sure. Now, let's go!"

In no time, Grim and Miles were climbing up the building. With the help of a fire-escape ladder, they made it up fairly quickly. From the roof, they were able to peer down on the theater. It was actually pretty cool.

"Wow, I don't think I've ever been up dis high," Miles sighed as he marveled at the view.   "The city almost looks pretty from up here."

"Yeah," Grim muttered softly, seemingly distracted by something else. "I mean, whatever."

"What is it, Grim?" Miles asked. "What's wrong?"

Grim pulled Miles closer, almost to the edge. "Look right there," he said, pointing down at the theater. "See that?"

"See what?" Miles squinted his eyes, but all he could see was the old building. As neat as it looked from way up there, he had no idea what Grim was pointing at. "I see the theater, is dat what you mean?"

"No, no, look this way," Grim pointed again, this time specifically at a bunch of bushes to the rear. "See that thing down there?"

"What thing? What?"

Grim brought Miles even closer to the edge of the building. Another step and they'd surely fall. "Look real close at that first bush.

Life Eight

What do you see just under it?"

Miles tried again. "Oh, yes! I think I saw someone!" Down below, there was a definite shape near the bush. As high as they were, Miles could make out a long tail and two pointy ears. Someone down there was hiding, but why?   "Who is that? Is it a Stick?"

"That's no Stick," Grim sighed. "It's an Alley." He took another long look down at the theater. "Do you know what, I see others! I can see at least five of them! What are they doing down there?"

"Any ideas?"

"I don't know, but they've got the place under surveillance!"

"This can't be good!" Miles cried. "But why?"

"I don't know," Grim said as he bit at his claws. "They must be angry, that's all I can figure."

"Angry at what?"

"Angry at the Sticks for keeping Fidel locked up."

"Oh, dat's right," Miles agreed. He leaned a tiny bit further over the building's edge, and then made another important discovery. "Look, Grim! It's Terrence and Roger! I see them!"

"Yes, I see them too!" Grim yelled. "I wonder if they see the Alleys!"

Things were getting very interesting down below. Like Grim suggested, the

Life Eight

Alleys had the theater surrounded. Watching Terrence and Roger sneak around was about as tense as something could be. At any moment, they could have easily been discovered. What a sight that would have been.

"What are we gonna do?" Miles asked, his voice plagued with worry. "If da Alleys see them, it'll be bad news for sure."

"Yes, yes I know," Grim agreed, still gnawing at his nails. "But what can we do? We can't just go down there. If they see either one of us, it's lights out kitty!"

"We can't just leave 'em there, can we?"

"We're going to have to," Grim decided. "But the Sticks. We have to warn the Sticks that the Alleys have the place surrounded! They've probably got some sort of evil plan to attack!"

"Do you think Fidel's involved?" Miles asked.

"I'm sure of it," Grim said under his breath. "But you were a member of the Silent Five. You know better than me how his mind works. What do you think he's up to?"

"I can't imagine, but I think you must be right," Miles began. "Dis is some sort of payback for locking him up. The Sticks should be worried. Oh, this isn't good."

"I'm not gonna let anything happen! I can't! I've got too many friends down there, even if they don't want to be my friend anymore."

179

Chapter Eighteen

Grim stepped away from the building's edge and slowly walked toward the center of the roof. He finally stopped and sat on a large, rusted metal pipe. With his head down, he let go a heavy sigh and closed his eyes. Full of concern, Miles approached.

"I wish I could go down there right now and warn them, but you know I can't," Miles said softy. "If those are Alleys, then I bet da Silent Five is involved. If they see me, Fidel will have my neck."

"I know, I can't ask you to do that," Grim said. "Let's go back to Maxi's and wait for Terrence and Roger. Hopefully they won't get caught. They'll probably go home and look for us. Besides, if they do get caught, I don't want to be standing here watching, do you?"

"No way!" Miles said. "Let's go wait at home. There's nothing we can do here."

"Yes, let's go," Grim replied. "I just hope they leave this place soon. I've got to get back to that hospital as quickly as I can. I just have such a sinking feeling, but I need to know the Sticks are safe before I go."

Grim and Miles headed back to Maxi's house. Along the way, they had to hide a couple of times when they saw other cats approaching. Finally, they made it safe and sound. As always, the place was in total disarray. It always amazed Grim that someone chose to live that way. It was worse than living in an alley.

While Miles slept somewhere in the back,

Life Eight

Grim sat on what was left of the front steps and waited for Terrence and Roger. He hoped against hope that they were all right. He prayed they'd have some news about the Alleys. Maybe he was wrong about them. Maybe they just wanted to see how the Sticks lived. But no, Grim knew the Alleys were far too warlike just to be curious about their lifestyle. It was more likely they were gearing up for full-blown war.

After about an hour, Grim started pacing back and forth in front of the house. There was no sign of Terrence or Roger. Without them, he couldn't go to the hospital to check on Dennis. He had planned on spending the night again, but couldn't bear the thought of leaving the Sticks in such danger. With every minute that passed, he was growing more and more tense. Then finally, Terrence and Roger came walking up the street.

"Terrence! Roger! You're back!" Grim cried. "You made it! You made it!"

"Of course, we're back," Terrence said. "What did you think happened?"

"I saw you two at the theater," Grim began, speaking very quickly. "I saw all those Alleys around the place. Tell me why they were there! Tell me they're not up to something bad!"

"We just went there to look for you," Terrence said, purposely ignoring Grim. "I thought I heard you say you were going over there to check on someone. Wasn't that true? Who was it you were looking for?"

"I was looking for Roger!" Grim explained.

Chapter Eighteen

"Now tell me what's going on at the theater!"

"Why were you looking for me?" Roger asked.

"Never mind that, just tell me!" Grim pleaded.

Roger glanced over at Terrence. "We've got to tell him," he said softly. Terrence let out a sigh and shrugged his shoulders.

"Tell me what? What is it?" Grim demanded.

"Okay, okay, I'll tell you," Terrence finally agreed. "I'll tell you." Once again, Terrence sighed. It was obvious he didn't have good news.

"It's true, the Alleys do have the place surrounded. They've got some crazy idea that they're going to lock in all the Sticks and basically starve them or something."

"What?" Grim blurted, his eyes wide as the sky.

"Yeah, but that's not the worst part," Terrence went on. "You see, the Alleys that I overheard said Fidel was going to come soon and get one of the Sticks."

"Which one? Tell me, who is he going to get?"

Terrence shot Roger a quick look for support. "Someone named Candle. Do you know anyone named Candle?"

Grim stepped back. His heart stopped. He put his paw to his chest. "Candle? Why does he want Candle? She's really an Alley. Why would he…"

 182

Life Eight

"They said something about revenge," Roger added. "For some reason, he's angry at her specifically. I don't know why. We had to leave. There were too many of them for us to stay."

"Roger, Fidel's your father," Terrence went on. "What do you think he's going to do?" Until that moment, Grim had forgotten that Roger was Fidel's son. His mind had been so busy with Dennis, that the very thought had slipped his mind.

"I don't know," Roger admitted. "You know him as well as me. He could do anything, really anything. The unfortunate thing is, I don't think there's anything we can do."

Grim shut his eyes. Memories of Candle flashed in his mind. She had always been so good to him, so selfless. Could he leave her now, now that he knew Fidel was coming for her? He didn't leave her to die when she was held captive in Vent City, and he wasn't going to leave her now.

"We've got to warn the Sticks!" Grim cried. "We've got to! They've got to get Candle out of there somehow. We've got to try!"

"But how are we going to warn them?" Terrence asked. "You said yourself that none of them can see you. They think you're already dead! If you show up looking like Grim, that would be even worse. They'll never listen to you. How are we going to pull this off?"

Grim began to pace again, faster and faster. The more he struggled to think of a plan,

Chapter Eighteen

the quicker he walked. Back and forth. Back and forth. Terrence and Roger just watched him. His face was deep in thought, and his breath was heavy. After a few moments, Grim stopped suddenly. "I've got it! Roger and Terrence!"

"What do we have do with this?" Roger asked.

"Nothing, but the Sticks won't recognize you." Grim turned to Terrence. "Terrence, nobody knows you. Not the Sticks or the Alleys. Miles and I are too much of a risk. It's you! You and Roger have to go find some Sticks and warn them. You've got to do it. It's the only way to save them!"

"You mean just wander around until we see someone?" Terrence asked. "And just walk right up to them? Won't they run away? Why would they listen to us?"

"Because you'll make them listen," Grim said. "Tell them who you are. Tell them you're Troop members who fought for them in the theater. Maybe they will recognize you. I don't care, you simply have to warn them! I can't let anything happen to Candle!"

Terrence stepped a little closer to Grim. "Who is this Candle anyway? She your girl or something?"

"No, no we're just friends," Grim said rather unconvincingly. "Sure, she's a girl, but it's not like that. Really, she's just a friend." Truth be told, Candle had never been just a friend. The two were bonded in a way most will never

 184

know. Even though they had some tough times together, she always would have a place in his heart. With as much conflict as he had going on in his life right now, he still wasn't willing to cast Candle aside. He had to help her.

"Let's go now," Grim continued. "I'll help you find some Sticks and then you can warn them. Then I must get back to that hospital. I simply have to find out what's going on with Dennis."

"Okay then," Terrence agreed. "Let's get going."

In no time, the three Troop members were up and running. With Miles awake and filled in on the situation, the gang headed off into the city looking for Sticks.

Chapter Nineteen

Grim, Miles, Terrence, and Roger walked up and down the cold city streets. Above them, the sky was its usual grey, just dark enough to tease everyone with the possibility of another all out storm. Because of this, the city was empty. Lifeless. Even the drabby, old buildings looked dead. Nothing ever got better in the city. Everything always seemed to only get worse.

"See anyone?" Roger asked.

"Nope, not yet," Terrence said, his eyes darting back and forth looking for any signs of life.

Grim was trying hard to focus, but his mind was at that hospital. The distraction was making him antsy. It was getting late, and he knew he simply must get back to Dennis's room. If anything were to happen to Dennis while he

 186

wasn't there, he'd never get over it.

"This seems kinda silly," Miles spoke up. "I mean, we don't even know who we're looking for. Don't you think there's a better way?"

Suddenly, Grim saw someone familiar just up the street. "Calvin!" Grim yelled. "I see Calvin! He's perfect!"

"What? Who's Calvin?" Terrence asked.

"Calvin's a Stick. We've got to talk to him right away!" A short distance ahead, Grim could clearly see his old friend. He was alone and apparently trying to attack a thin rope that was hanging off a store awning. Calvin was always a little bit odd, most actors are. Still, it was good to see him.

"Well, let's give it a try," Terrence said.

While Grim and Miles stayed out of sight, Roger and Terrence walked over to him. "Tell him to warn the Sticks," Grim cried in a whisper as they trotted off. "Tell him he's got to hurry."

Terrence glanced back at Grim as he and Roger approached Calvin. Calvin, who was still tugging at that rope, hadn't noticed the two strange cats walking toward him. Standing a safe distance away, Grim and Miles watched nervously. Finally, Roger and Terrence were just inches from Calvin.

"Um, excuse me, sir," Terrence said politely. "Sir? Can I have a word with you?"

Startled, Calvin let go of the rope and flew into a combat stance. His tail bloomed and his ears perked into perfect little peaks. "Who are you? What do you want from me?" He put up his two front paws and as threateningly as he could, waved them in front of his face.

"We just need to talk," Roger said. "No one wants to hurt you."

"Talk about what?" Calvin snarled. "I don't know you! Are you Alleys?"

"No, we're not Alleys," Roger began. "We're Troop members."

"Troops? I don't know what the Troops are!" Calvin yelled. "I'm getting out of here! I'm not stupid!"

Calvin started to walk away. Grim watched anxiously from the shadows, hoping Terrence or Roger would intercept. Luckily, they did.

"You need to warn the Sticks at the theater!" Terrence yelled.

Calvin stopped. "What?" he cried.

"I said, you need to go to the theater and warn the Sticks."

"Warn them about what?" Now Calvin seemed a little more interested. "How do I know this isn't a trick?" Grim bit his claws as he listened from a safe distance.

"The Alleys have the place surrounded," Roger explained in an excited voice. "They're mad at you guys for keeping Fidel all chained up! He's going to come and get Candle if you don't do something!"

Calvin took a hesitant step closer. "Like I said, how do I know you're telling the truth? I've got a plane to catch that will fly me out west for

 188

a big movie job. I'm not going to miss it because of you two."

"This isn't a trick!" Terrence pleaded. "It's the truth! Candle will be taken or worse! You've got to go warn them! Now!"

Calvin wasn't convinced. His extensive Stick training taught him to always be on guard. "Naw, I'm outta here. How do I know you guys aren't quacks? This doesn't make any sense." He turned his back on them and started to walk away. "Later!"

Terrence and Roger stood dumbfounded as the blood began to drain from their bodies. They looked at each other with worry. This hadn't gone as they had expected.

Calvin was nearly around the corner when Grim suddenly came charging forward. "Calvin, wait!" he called. "Calvin, stop! It's me, Romeo!"

Calvin froze in his tracks, his back to the others. Grim waited nervously for him to turn around, his heart pounding. Calvin hesitated, but after a few long seconds, he turned. "Romeo? Romeo, is that really you?" Calvin stared wide-eyed at Grim. "How's that…I mean, is it really….I mean, aren't you dead?"

Grim slowly walked closer. He held out his paw to keep the others at bay. He knew he had just taken a big risk, but if it meant helping Candle, it was worth it. "Yes, it is me, Calvin. I know this seems impossible, but well, I did survive the accident in Grimsville."

"Why didn't you tell us?" Calvin asked,

looking as though he had just seen a ghost. "Why did you lie?"

"Well, the hot oil left me deformed, and I saw it as a new beginning for me. I was angry and I wanted to disappear. I started going by the name Grim. It was they only way I could save myself during a big rainstorm. I convinced the Alleys I was Grim, and they got sucked in."

"Sucked in? What do you mean by that?"

"I became an Alley for a little while," Grim explained, "but it wasn't because I wanted to, it was because I had to. You may have seen me fighting alongside the Alleys at the theater."

"That was you? With the Alleys?" Calvin couldn't believe what he was hearing. "Romeo, have you gone mad?"

"Like I said, I had to," Grim explained. "It's all very complicated. Second, the name's Grim. But anyway, I'll tell you my whole sordid story another time. Now, you have to believe me, I'm not with the Alleys. What my friends said is right. You have to listen to them. The theater is surrounded. Fidel's going to get Candle, probably take her to his dungeon. You've got to warn the others!"

"But Romeo, I mean Grim," Calvin said, "if the theater is surrounded, what can I possibly do? They'll just get me, won't they?"

Grim hadn't thought of that. In fact, he hadn't thought this through much at all. His mind was still at the hospital, still hoping Dennis was getting better. "You're right, Calvin," he finally said. "I can't ask you to do that, not with all those Alleys out there."

"Well, that's a relief," Calvin sighed. "I've got a big job out west you know? I'm leaving on a plane tonight! Out west! The big time! It finally happened!"

"Out west?" Grim shrieked. "Did you hear a word I said?"

"Sure I did, but you even said there's nothing I can do."

Grim was at a loss. He didn't know what to do. Candle's fate was hanging delicately in his paws, and if he didn't think of something, she could die forever.

Just as Grim was about to send Calvin on his way, Roger came running toward them. "I heard what you said, and I think I know a way we can help."

"What is it, Roger?" Grim roared. "Tell me, please!"

"Well, my dad used to take me to that theater when us males were little kittens. He left us there alone one time when he went out hunting for something," he explained. Of course, Roger's father was none other than Fidel. "So, my brothers and I found this old pipe under the stage. I crawled in it on a dare, and it led out to one of the sewage pipes down the street. I'm sure I could get into the theater if I can find that pipe."

Grim reached over and put his two front paws on Roger's shoulders. "Why didn't you say something about that before?"

"I guess I forgot about it until now."

"Boy Grim, I can't wait until the others see you," Calvin blurted. "Won't they be surprised?"

"No! You can't tell them about me!" Grim warned. "Not yet."

"Why? What's the big deal?" Calvin asked.

"I'm just not ready," Grim sighed as his mind wandered to more difficult times. "They'll think I'm a traitor. I'm just not ready for that, so please don't say anything." He looked at Calvin, and Calvin understood. The seriousness and the fear in Grim's eyes said it all.

"Okay, I won't tell," Calvin assured. "Now, can I get home? We're leaving for the airport soon. Lloyd will be looking for me. He probably already is."

"Yes, of course. Now everybody, come closer!" Grim bellowed. "I've got the plan."

Everyone huddled together. "What's it gonna be?" Miles asked. He had stayed quiet all this time, finding the whole Grim-Romeo thing fascinating.

"All right, here's what's going to happen," Grim began. "Roger, you and Terrence go find that pipe and warn the Sticks. It's possible the Alleys know about it, so get out of there as soon as you can, got it?"

"Sure, we got it," Terrence said.

"Good, now Calvin, you head home. I know how important your big break is," Grim said with a smile. "Knock 'em dead out there."

"Sure, Grim. I will."

"Miles, why don't you head back to Maxi's and wait for Terrence and Roger," Grim went on. "If they don't return in one hour, gather the Troops and head to the theater. Get those Alleys out of there!"

"And what about you, Grim?" Miles asked. "Where are you gonna be?"

Grim looked up into the grey, afternoon sky. "I'm going back to the hospital. I have to see Dennis. I have to know he's all right."

"But didn't you just see him?" Miles asked. "Didn't you say he was doing fine?"

"Something the doctor said about head injuries being very serious," Grim mumbled to himself. "It scared me. I've got a bad feeling, and I've got to go back."

"Okay, but we better see you back at Maxi's by morning, okay?" Terrence insisted.

"Okay," Grim agreed. "Okay, everyone get on your way. It's going to be an interesting night. Be careful Roger and Terrence. Please be very careful."

Roger and Terrence nodded, then walked off in the direction of the theater. Miles turned and headed toward Maxi's, and Calvin was about to walk away when he had an idea. "Hey, Grim," he began, feeling strange about not calling him Romeo. "Why don't you come with me? I know how you love adventures."

"First of all, I don't love adventures, and

secondly, I'm staying at the hospital tonight," Grim explained. "You remember Dennis, well he's been hurt, and I have to stay with him. It's something I've got to do. Then, I need to check on Candle. I can't let anything happen to her."

"Awe, those other guys will take care of her," Calvin nagged. "Come with me. It's only for a little while, then we can come back."

"I can't exactly just walk onto an airplane, now can I?"

"I don't care what you say," Calvin teased. "You're Romeo Crumb, and Romeo Crumb can do anything he puts his mind to!"

Grim glared back at him. "Thanks, but no thanks, Calvin. You go off and do your movie, and I'll be waiting right here."

"Tell you what, I'll come by the hospital in one hour," Calvin said. "If you change your mind, I'll be waiting outside. I hope you're there."

"You know Calvin, you and I have never been great friends," Grim reminded. "Why the sudden interest in taking me along?"

"Oh, I don't know," Calvin wondered. "I guess I've changed."

"Well, good luck on your trip, and maybe I'll see you when you get back."

"The hospital," Calvin murmured to Grim. "I'll be waiting at the hospital. One hour."

"Bye." Grim shook his head and walked off. He wasn't lying. He had no intention of joining him on that airplane, as tempting as

 194

Life Eight

heading west sounded. He'd done enough running. The Sticks had always been told that the west was the ultimate paradise. A cat's dream. But for Grim, the only dream he had was in knowing Dennis and Candle were safe and well. So finally, after waiting nearly all day, Grim rushed back to the hospital. He couldn't wait to get there.

Chapter Twenty

Halfway to the hospital, it started to rain. The temperature dropped rapidly, and the threat of more hail filled the air. Grim was almost there, but he knew he had to hustle. That sky wasn't going to wait for anyone.

At last, Grim's four paws were on the hospital lawn. He looked up at the large building. Bright flashes of light flickered on and off. The news crews had returned, and they were in the building.

Grim entered the hospital in the same way he had before. Soon, he was back on Dennis's floor, inching his way down the hallway. Unfortunately the place was much busier than it had been the night before, but luckily for him everyone was preoccupied. They hadn't noticed him yet.

Life Eight

Grim could see Dennis's room up ahead. C23, just like before. It was early evening now, and Grim hoped Dennis and the other boy would be getting their nightly meds soon. Just the thought of Dennis all loopy again made him smile.

Outside of Dennis's room were several cameramen. A fairly large crowd had gathered in the hallway. Grim stayed back, hiding himself under a computer cart. *Maybe I came back too soon,* he thought. *It's too crowded now. I'll be spotted for sure!*

Grim saw Mrs. Crumb at the center of the crowd. She looked worried and distraught. He knew it must have been hard visiting Dennis at the hospital with cameras in her face. But why were they there now? Had things changed? Did Dennis take a turn for the worse? Grim leaned against C23's wall and listened as closely as he could.

"Mrs. Crumb, can we talk in private please?" the doctor asked. "Away from all these cameras?"

"Well, of course, doctor," she answered. Grim noticed she had the same exact clothes on as the day before. The only difference was the creases in them. "But when can I see Dennis? He's just right in there." She pointed at the door to Dennis's room, which was blocked by reporters.

"This way, Mrs. Crumb," the doctor said as he led her to an empty room. "We can talk in here."

Chapter Twenty

The reporters all tried to follow them, but the doctor shut the door just in time. Of course, he hadn't realized somebody did get in...Grim. Standing behind a large trashcan, he waited and listened.

"Mrs. Crumb," the doctor slowly began.

"Yes, doctor?" Her voice shook nervously.

"Mrs. Crumb, as you know we are doing everything possible for Dennis." With one hand to her shoulder, he looked deeply in her eyes, fluffed his finely gelled hair, and continued. "As I told you earlier, sometimes things happen with head injuries. Now, while Dennis was doing fine earlier, we saw something on the scan we took this afternoon."

"Scan? What scan?" Mrs. Crumb cried, flustered and shaking. "What did you find? What?"

Grim's heart was pounding so loudly, he thought for sure the doctor and Mrs. Crumb could hear it. He began to sweat, and his mouth was suddenly very dry. The news was bad, just as he had imagined.

"We saw a small spot on his brain, so it could be nothing, but it could be something. In his usual patronizing way, the doctor added, "We'll just have to see after the surgery what's going to happen next."

"Surgery? He needs surgery?"

"Oh, yes, just a little surgery," the doctor said. "Nothing to worry about. We just need to crack open his skull and..."

Life Eight

Mrs. Crumb fell to the floor. Her little clutch purse shot across the room, and the heel from one of her plum colored pumps flung in the opposite direction.

Feeling a rush of adrenalin, Grim burst out of that hospital room and dashed for C23. He didn't care in that moment who saw him or what happened. But that was a decision he'd soon regret.

Grim plowed though the crowd of people outside Dennis's room. He got knocked around a bit from all the people, but in a matter of seconds had found himself inside. Hustling to the other side of the room, he was finally next to Dennis.

Dennis was either asleep or unconscious. Either way, he wasn't moving. There was a nurse inside, along with two reporters. Allowing his body to take over, Grim jumped onto Dennis's bed.

"We just have to prep him for surgery," the nurse said to the reporter. "He'll be going in just a few…"

When the nurse suddenly stopped talking, Grim knew he had been spotted.

"Ahhh! There's a cat in here! A cat!" she wailed.

"Get a picture! Get a picture!" one of the cameramen shouted. "Hurry!"

"Front page news, *'Cat visits boy on deathbed!'* I can see it now!" cried the other.

Deathbed? Deathbed? Grim screamed in his head. *Not a chance!*

Chapter Twenty

As the nurse continued to holler and the cameramen readied their cameras, Dennis awoke. He opened his tired, bloodshot eyes, and standing on his chest, clear as a bell, was his old cat Romeo.

"Romeo! You're back! You're back!" Dennis cried, struggling to sit up. "It wasn't just a dream! You're really real!"

For a moment, everything else in the room seemed to go silent. It was just Dennis and Grim, two best friends. But eventually, that had to end. The entire hospital staff and all those reporters came exploding into the room. Grim knew he had to get out, but how?

"Get that cat! Somebody grab him!" the people were shouting.

"Don't let him get away! Grab him! Grab him!"

But Grim wasn't going to let that happen. He was not about to go to the Pound and risk being in there for Dennis's surgery. He searched quickly for a way out, as the crowd grew closer and closer.

Grim hissed as hard as he could. He held up his sharp claws and stretched his mouth to show his long, pointy teeth. But try as he might, he still didn't see a way out. If he made a run for it, they'd grab him for sure. There were just too many people standing around.

"Romeo! I'm so glad you're here!" Dennis cried again. He reached his frail arms up to grab him, but as he did, one of the reporters got in the way. Grim had no choice but to jump off the bed. It was then he noticed the open window.

Jumping up to the window ledge, Grim looked over the side. It was a long drop, suicide for sure. Still, it was the chance he had to take. The Pound was not an alternative. Not now. Not ever.

Grim stood on that ledge, gripping the wall with one paw, and holding the other high and menacingly. He looked at Dennis, and with as much expression as a cat can make, he nodded goodbye.

"Romeo, don't!" Dennis screamed. But it was too late. Grim had jumped. Falling three stories was a feat some cats could survive, but not this time. Grim lay dead in a puddle of his own blood...again. Without the knowledge of living nine lives, he would have never done it, but given the circumstances, he had to try.

Grim didn't know it, but a barrage of cameras had photographed the whole thing. Five or six of them had squeezed themselves into that open window and were photographing his lifeless body as he lay motionless on the ground. After a few minutes, they went back inside, and the buzz continued in the hospital room.

Calvin, who promised to be there, had seen the whole thing. Never being the brightest Stick in the bunch, Calvin knew he couldn't leave Grim just lying there. "You're coming with me," he whispered in Grim's ear.

With Grim's neck held tightly in Calvin's

mouth, Calvin began to drag Grim home. Luckily by then, the cameras had turned back to Dennis. The streets were still deserted, as the storm was just about ready to unleash its wrath. Calvin knew time was of the essence. It would be a lot more difficult for him to carry his friend in the rain. So he pushed on, pulling him as carefully and as quickly as he could.

Along the way, Calvin spotted Terrence and Roger as they came running up the street. Calvin put Grim on the ground and yelled, "Hey, fellas! It's me, Calvin, remember? From before!"

Terrence and Roger stopped. They saw Grim lying there, and they knew he was dead. "What happened to him?" Terrence shouted. "How did this happen?"

"He jumped out the window!" Calvin cried. "I don't know why? Luckily, I was there waiting for him!"

"We were just heading for the hospital to find him!" Roger explained. "We need to tell him what happened!"

Calvin suddenly remembered the other obstacle of the day. Carrying Grim, he had nearly forgotten. "Oh, my! What happened at the theater? Did you get Candle? Is everything all right?"

Still a little out of breath, Terrence cried, "We went through the pipe, just like Roger said, but when we got there...Fidel..."

"Fidel is my father," Roger admitted again. "When we got there the Sticks were all in a frenzy. Fidel had just been there. He and the Alleys came in. They got Candle! They took her away!"

"We need Grim to wake up from this death so he can go get her!" Terrence wailed. "All the Troops will help! We'll do it together!"

Suddenly, Calvin's face changed. He seemed angry and determined. "Grim's coming with me! He needs a vacation! I'm taking him out west!"

"You can't!" Roger yelled. "That's a crazy idea! He's got to stay! There's too much at stake!"

"Just watch me!" Calvin hollered as he opened up and gripped Grim's neck once again. With surprising stamina and strength, he rushed off with Grim held tightly in his mouth, disappearing into the night. Terrence and Roger were left standing. They'd have to get Candle without him.

A couple hours later, Grim finally opened his eyes. Everything was blurry. He took in a deep breath, trying hard to figure out where he was. All he could hear was a very loud, whooshing noise that he couldn't explain other than to say he had never heard it before. The air was stale, and he found it somewhat hard to breath.

His eyes were finally beginning to adjust. As they did, he was able to see Calvin standing beside him. It was then he realized he was in a box, a cat carrier box. Feeling his body go into panic mode, Grim looked around some more. To his left, he could see out of the crate. Just beyond

that was a tiny window. Grim hopped up on his hind legs, crouching down and struggling to see out. When he saw the large wing, he knew he was on an airplane.

"What have you done?" he snarled back at Calvin. "Are you crazy? You kidnapped me! Now I'll never know if Dennis is alive!"

Grim leaned in closer toward the window. They were high in the air, but below the clouds. Grim took a good look at the city below him.

"We are now approaching West Airport," spoke a voice over the loud speaker. "If you look out your window, you'll be able to see what a beautiful, sunny day it is. Please prepare for arrival."

In that moment, something unexplainable came over Grim. All the drama of his lives seemed to suddenly melt away. Even the idea of Dennis in surgery or Candle taken by Fidel had slid to the farthest corners of his mind. With a huge grin in Calvin's direction, Grim settled back down, excited to get out of there and live like he had never lived before. The only question now was, how much more living would there be? He knew he had to be careful because... Romeo Crumb was finally a niner.

L. RIFKIN

THE NINE LIVES OF
RomeoCrumb

LIFE ONE

L. RIFKIN
THE NINE LIVES OF
Romeo Crumb
LIFE ONE

In the garbage filled alleys of a once great city exists a society of cats held captive under the wicked claw of a ferocious tyrant. Will one of them be able to face the ultimate villain and free his fellow felines, even if it takes his nine lives to do it?

Stratford Road
Press, Ltd.

L. RIFKIN

THE NINE LIVES OF
RomeoCrumb

LIFE TWO

L. RIFKIN
THE NINE LIVES OF
Romeo Crumb
LIFE TWO

Fidel has a plan. A nasty plan that could destroy the hope of an entire society of cats and raise him to the peaks of power. Will Fidel's evil plan succeed? Or will Romeo and the Sticks at last find peace in the city they call home? One thing is certain, through all the chaos and turmoil, a new leader is born.

Stratford Road
Press, Ltd.

L. RIFKIN

THE NINE LIVES OF
RomeoCrumb

LIFE THREE

L. RIFKIN
THE NINE LIVES OF
Romeo Crumb
LIFE THREE

Beneath the depressed city where no cat has dared to go before, a nation of grotesque mutants hides afraid to show their melted faces to the outside world. Sentenced to their life of darkness by Fidel, will the mutants finally emerge from their underground prison to join the Sticks in battling their common enemy? Will Romeo lead the charge against the evil Alleys of is he too sick to fight? Perhaps an unexpected visitor will have the answer.

Stratford Road
Press, Ltd.

THE NINE LIVES OF
RomeoCrumb

LIFE FOUR

L. RIFKIN
THE NINE LIVES OF
Romeo Crumb
LIFE FOUR

With the monsterous Fidel gone from their lives, the Sticks have flourished like never before, but the good times are short lived as a new enemy emerges. Dozens of angry, mutant rats drive Romeo to his mental limit spinning him into a state of near delirium. Exhausted, he must meet the rats' unjust demands or face the consequences. Will a series of haunting events stand in his way, or will Romeo triumph over evil once again?

Stratford Road
Press, Ltd.

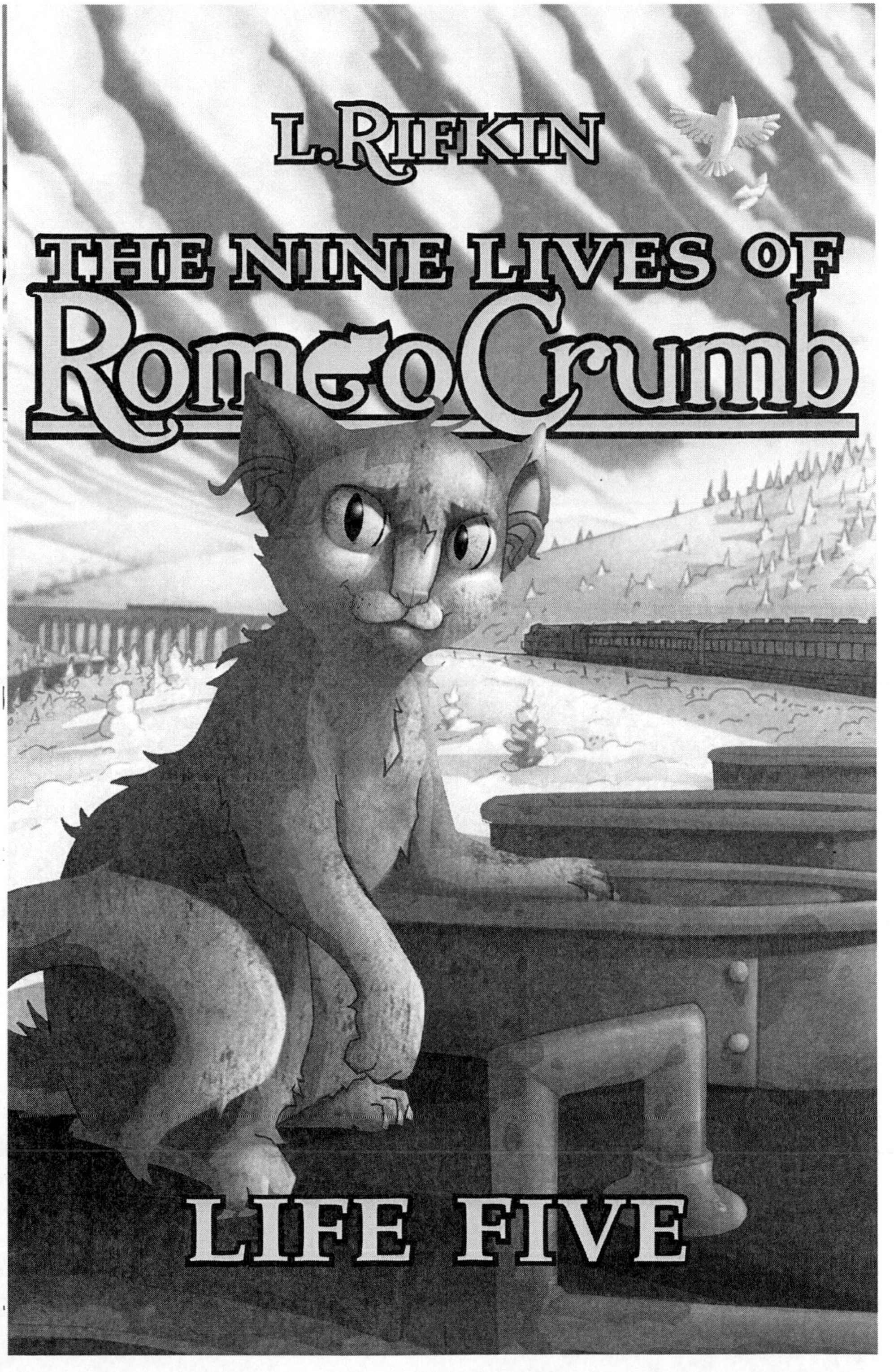
L. RIFKIN
THE NINE LIVES OF
Romeo Crumb
LIFE FIVE

L. RIFKIN
THE NINE LIVES OF
Romeo Crumb
LIFE FIVE

On the run, Romeo hops a train and heads west to escape the pressures of his troubled life. All seems well until the train is involved in a horrific wreck. Unharmed, Romeo stumbles into Grimsville, a charming, nearby town and just the haven Romeo needs to snap him out of his funk. Plentiful food, warm sunshine, and some surprise visitors keep Romeo wondering if he should ever return to the city at all. But just as Romeo is about to embrace his newfound happiness, Grimsville has one final surprise up its sleeve.

Stratford Road
Press, Ltd.

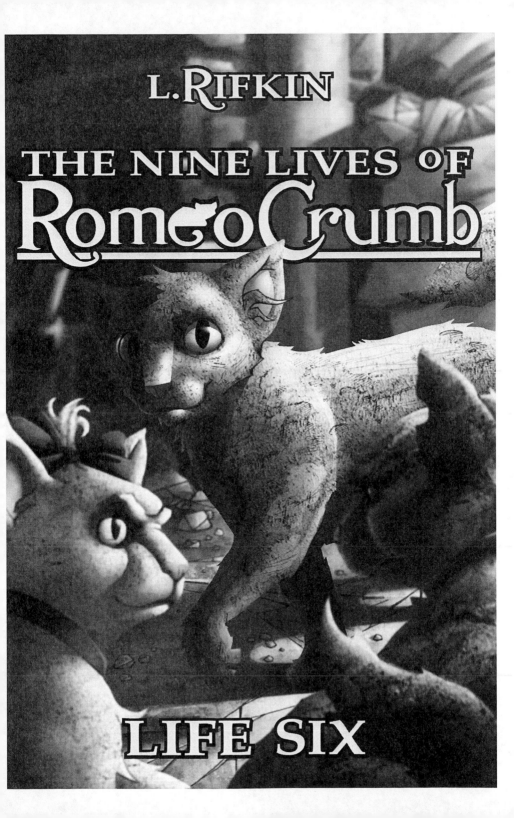

L. RIFKIN
THE NINE LIVES OF
Romeo Crumb
LIFE SIX

Romeo's adventures outside the city have failed in the worst possible way leaving him grossly disfigured. In spite of his tragic misfortune, Romeo is eager to begin again only to return to a city he doesn't recognize, and more distressing, a city that doesn't recognize him. In a bizarre twist of fate, Romeo finds his only refuge living life as an Alley cat in the dreaded Fourth Corner. With a new name and identity, Romeo wonders just how long it will be before Fidel realizes who he really is.

Stratford Road
Press, Ltd.